GOLD DIGGERS
&
THIMBLERIGGERS

Donncha Ó Sullivan

ORIGINAL WRITING

ISBNS
Parent : 978-1-78237-450-3
epub: 978-1-78237-451-0
mobi: 978-1-78237-452-7
PDF: 978-1-78237-453-4

A cip catalogue for this book is available from the National Library.

Published by Original Writing Ltd., Dublin, 2013.

Printed by Clondalkin Group, Glasnevin, Dublin 11

For Mary

Acknowledgements

I must thank my family and my many friends, too numerous to list, just for being there throughout my wilderness years and beyond.

CONTENTS

Chapter One

IT'S NOT EASY SKIN

The German jigger hit something hard. So hard it rebounded from the tunnel face. The tool struck the miner behind it like the recoil from a shotgun, almost dislocating his shoulder.

"Fuck it, what in the Christ is that?" grunted The Badger Boyle.

He withdrew the tool and cleared away the debris and muck in front of him. He was some 30 metres into the tunnel and had at least another 30 metres to go before hitting the reception shaft.

"London Clay all the way" the Engineer had said and so it had been this far.

They were excavating the tunnel the old fashioned way, using hand tools. The tunnel had an internal diameter of 1.5 metres. The walls were concrete lined, built up in segments into rings behind the tunnel shield as it was jacked forward into the excavated face.

The Badger used a mattock to pull away the stiff soil from the obstruction. He expected to find he had hit a cobble or boulder even though such were rare in this type of ground. There weren't any sewers or services at this depth and the nearest Underground Line was the Central Line over fifty metres away so it couldn't be that. They could hear the trains rumbling in the distance as they worked.

"What could that be Phil?" he said again to his shovel man, Phil Doherty.

"Fucked if I know!" said Phil – "here, take another skelp out of it and we'll have a look."

The Badger took up the jigger and worked the loose soil away, revealing a concrete mass of some sort at the left hand side of the tunnel face. It looked to be the outside corner of a basement or similar. The concrete was cracked where Boyle had hit it.

"You better call Dónal down" said The Badger. "He'll get a claim out of this and we'll get paid for doing fuck-all while the suits sort it out. Mark my words."

"Wait a minute wait a minute" said Phil "crack open that wall and we'll see what's behind it first."

The Badger took up the tool, a Hauser H11, the Magnum 44 of mining tools. In the right hands it would make short work of any concrete or rock and The Badger had the right hands. After a couple of bursts he had a small fissure opened. A couple of bursts more he had a hole made and widened.

He worked the jigger point into the concrete. It was strong stuff, old, fully cured and as hard as iron but bit by bit he opened it up until it was about third of a metre wide and twice that in depth when he stopped.

"I reckon we're coming to the end of it – the jigger's ringing hollow" he shouted.

"How the fuck would you know?" said Phil, "you're as deaf as a post!"

"I can feel it you bollox. There's something hollow behind it. And you can't talk! Your hearing is worse than mine – I don't know why you bother sticking plugs into them big ugly lugs of yours. You should have been shoving them into your ear holes years ago, before the damage was done."

"Ha? What's that?" said Phil and they both laughed. Deafness is an occupational hazard in tunnelling. Working with loud, noisy equipment in confined spaces, for long periods, often in a compressed air environment, played havoc with the eardrums.

There were very few miners who hadn't suffered some hearing loss but the money was good and as young men going into the game they had seen earplugs as either a hindrance or a nuisance. As a result most tunnelling veterans had serious hearing difficulties.

Tony Boyle, nicknamed The Badger, partly because of his salt and pepper hair and partly because of his ability to burrow, gave the jigger a few more shots of air and the resistance gave way. He drew the tool back and shone his torch into the space ahead. It looked like they had burst into a room or a cellar of some sort. But they were at least six metres below the foundation level of the nearest building.

"You've done it now, you're after breaking into a basement!" Phil shouted.

"Basement my arse! We're 30 foot below any building here. Come out of there and we'll call Dónal down when we go for a bite."

The alarm on the gas detector sounded the "Low Oxygen" alert. The Badger turned it off, ignoring the warning.

"That'll be from the stale air inside" he said as he sparked up the half cigarette hanging from his lip. Smoking was strictly prohibited underground. The risk of explosion should they hit a pocket of trapped gas was too high. These men paid little heed to such rules however. They knew by the nature of the face whether there was a risk of gas just as they could smell water ahead. And it was water they feared more than any gas. Hit an underground stream or perched water and that tunnel would be flooded back to the drive shaft in no time.

Phil had been at the face when he undermined a canal one time. The force of the water had carried him all the way back the tunnel and into the shaft. He only got out by grabbing hold of the crane cable. Had the crane driver been asleep or out of his cab for one reason or another Phil would have been a goner. He couldn't swim and he would have drowned as the water cascaded into the shaft, flooding it. As it happened the driver was alert and raised the crane jib straight up, yanking Phil out of the pit.

"Come on," The Badger said again, "we'll go up and have the breakfast and we'll see what we'll do."

The two men walked, knees bent, in a stoop peculiar to miners, back to the drive shaft, drawing fresh air into their lungs as they advanced. They emerged from the tunnel into the open air. Both men stood upright for the first time in three hours and stretched.

"I'm getting too old for this lark. I reckon I have lumbago. Between backache and arthritis and miner's white finger I have nothing but pains and aches."

"It's not easy skin" said Phil.

"No one said it was going to be easy" replied the Badger.

"Sure if it was easy everyone would be at it" retorted Phil.

They laughed as if this was the first time these words were uttered and heard even though they had the same conversation each time they exited the hole. They climbed the vertical ladder, having the crack all the way up as ever, The Badger going ahead and farting in the general direction of the following Phil.

"You dirty bastard, what were you drinking last night? You're rotten – I swear something just crawled out of your arse and died."

"Serves you right – you dropped a few stinkers in the tunnel yourself only I was too polite to comment. Heineken I'd say."

"No - loose porter! Rotten, or what? I was sure I'd set the Gas Detector off down below. I had a couple of rums as well."

On reaching the top landing, each man removed his name tag from the "in" hook and placed it on the "out" hook. The Badger placed the battery of the Gas Detector in the charger while Phil switched off the plant. He checked the fuel tanks in the compressor and in the pumps to make sure the lads had filled them up that morning. These routine jobs done, they headed for the toilets and washed off as much of the morning's muck as they could before heading for the tea hut for the best part of the day, the breakfast.

For most people, breakfast is a light morning repast, taken in comfortable surroundings at home. For many others it is taken in a restaurant or café. Construction workers in general use roadside caffs or site canteens but tunnel wokers traditionally have their meals in their own gang huts. The nature of the work is such that miners are seldom able to get cleaned up properly before they eat. The thirty minute break is simply too short. Also, miners need an enormous intake of calories to sustain them through four hours at the face. Even the biggest site canteen breakfast isn't enough for these guys.

The crews have a kitty and one of the crew, the youngest usually, is charged with the job of 'shackling up', or buying the food and cooking it. The main ingredients are steak and eggs and refried potatoes. A few sausages, puddings and rashers are thrown into the mix and the lot is dished up with copious amounts of baked beans and sliced white bread. Several mugs of tea are drunk to wash the feast down.

Not much is said while the men are eating. There will always be some complaint about the cook, the price or the quality, but the food is polished off every morning without fail.

Carbohydrates and high energy foods are the order of the day here. Yet there are no fat miners! Every bit of lard is burned off before it gets a chance to settle.

"The folks who go to weightwatchers could do with spending a few shifts down below" the miners would often say.

Once the main body of the meal is finished, the men give themselves over to a quiet period of rest. The only sounds to be heard in the hut during this ten minutes are from the occasional belch or fart, (followed by laughs and cries of "get out you bastard"). The tabloids are flicked through and the regulation comments passed on the half naked models displaying their assets therein.

Billy Halloran, the crane driver and self appointed horseracing expert, a man who could tell you the winner of every classic race for the past ten years and give you the names of the jockeys, trainers and owners of the winning horses to boot, opened the daily racing preview cum comment.

"That fucker Aidan O'Brien is at it again – he had two horses in a race at Doncaster yesterday. One went off at 6 to 4 favourite and the other one was an outsider at 12 to one. He had his son who is only an apprentice claiming 4lbs on the outsider while he put Murtagh on the jolly. There was money for the outsider at the off and the fucker won by three lengths in a five furlong race. Backed in from 33 to 20 and returned at 12s. The poor old punter hasn't a chance."

"Had you it backed Billy?" asked Phil.

"No. No. I backed Murtagh's mount. I put £40 on the nose. The useless bastard!"

"A fool and his money are easily parted. Aren't we sick and tired of telling you the whole thing is one big fiddle? Dónal will tell you that. And he knows. He used to get great information from up North one time. He knew a fellow who was connected. Here he is now – ask him yourself."

"Dónal, will you tell that eegit about backing horses?"

Their Site Agent, Dónal Byrne, had come into the cabin.

"Good morning chaps" he said "what fettle?", as he lifted a cold sausage from the table and bit into it.

"Horses? "he continued. "don't talk to me about horses. The only people who make money at that crack are the bookies and the trainers. I should know. A mate of mine is renting a property to Paddy Powers Bookmakers for ten years or more – they never once missed the rent – punters like Billy pay for that!"

"A bookie's license is a license to print money. Make no mistake about it! The poor old working sod hasn't a chance. Neither does the horse owner half of the time. Do you remember that job we did in Cumbria? Do you remember I stayed in a pub up there? The landlord was a Freemason – you know, one of the guys with the funny handshakes. He was friendly with half the trainers up North – they're all masons as well. They used to give my man the real lowdown on their nags."

"I was only there a week when he said to me – I'll never forget it – he had a stutter – 'dd ddd do you follow the horses Dónal? I never met an Irishman yet who dddidn't" says he. 'I like a bet' says I.

'Wwww Well' he says 'there's one out today that will win at a nice price and two others who will dddefinitely be trying.' And there's a fff favourite in the third race in Newton Abbott that won't be making any effort at all. The second in the bbbetting will probably wwwwin that one.'

'Come on' he says 'we'll go into the bbbbookies in Barrow – the local bookie in Millom won't take my bets over the phone anymore – he closed the account on account of me ringing in bbbets at the off.'

The horse he said would win was priced at nine to one and the two triers were priced at fives and sevens. I did an each way round robin – the bet cost me ninety snots – that was a lot for me then. Richard, the landlord did the same bet but he laid out

two hundred and seventy. The three nags came in and I cleared
nearly two grand! Richard cleared eight.

I wanted to back a few more as my luck was in but my man
was having none of it.

'Luck had nowt to do with it' he said 'put your winnings in
your pppocket until the next time.'

I gave the rest of the day and the following day on the beer
– I spent the bones of a year up there and I never touched my
wages for weeks at a time. He would ring me up on my mobile
"are yyyou anywhere near a bbbookies Don?" he'd say, "well
if you are then pppop in and have a bbbet on such and such."
Happy days!

I blew the winnings of course – flat out boozing and chasing
women! I had three on the go at one time. One down in
Southampton, one near Manchester and one in Cumbria. How
did I get started on that? Oh yeah, Billy and his bet – take it
from me Billy, if you're not in the know, backing horses is a
mug's game. I must give Richard a bell one of these days. I lost
touch with him when I went to the Middle East. Is there any tea
going? How many did ye get yesterday?"

"Four rings, same as the day before" came the reply, "and
we'll not get any more in that ground, before you ask." The
Badger waited until the others were out of the hut, leaving
Dónal and himself alone.

"We found something down below Dónal" he said "you have
to come down and see. It looks like an old concrete basement or
something. I didn't say a word to anyone. Only Phil and myself
seen it. We only hit it in the past hour."

"Don't talk to me about any shagging basement Tony. We
won't make a shilling on this job at four rings a shift. It was
priced at that. We have to get five rings to make it pay. I've seen
the figures. Fallon will blow a fuse. We'll have to put a night
shift on and that'll be a disaster.

You know me well enough to know I'm not bullshitting.
You have to get five rings! The measure is due at the end of the
month and we need to be hitting the other side of the drive or

we're all in the shit. It's alright for you, Tony, you won't have to talk to Fallon – It'll be me getting the bollocking!"

Ned Fallon was the Contracts Manager for Kingdom Tunnelling, the firm they all worked for. It was only a small company and it was dodgy, just like every tunnelling outfit, only more so than most. The company was under resourced and run on a shoestring for the benefit of its owner, Jim Corbett. Unlike his namesake though, this Jim Corbett was no gentleman.

Corbett had maybe sixty or so workers at the most and had a well earned reputation for trickiness. Suppliers wouldn't deal with him unless he paid cash up front for goods and services and main contractors were wary of him because he was always on the lookout for a claim or an extra something or other. But tunnelling is a niche market so they needed him as much as he needed them.

"A symbiotic relationship" was how Dónal thought of it.

The one thing Corbett had going for him was that, come hell or high water, the wages were paid, in cash and on time every week. Because of that and only because of that his men got the work done.

"We'll get the fifth ring all right but only if there's something in it for us" said The Badger. "Another £200 per shift between the two at the face and we'll sort the lads out with a drink if they have to stay on an hour or so to help with the grouting. I meant it when I said we hit something though. Come on down for a look."

"Fuck you", said Dónal, "you're never happy unless you get me into the hole. I was out late last night. I should be going for a cure now and writing up my diary in some pub or other. I want an easy life – all you do is give me grief – you better not be having me on you bollox. I'll get you the bonus but you better deliver or Fallon will put Maguire in on nights and we don't that fucker around the place."

The two men descended the ladder.

"Where were you at it last night Dónal? There's a fair stink of booze from you" The Badger said, "you better suck some zubes before you go back to the office. The Resident Engineer will have you off the job if he thinks you have drink taken – he had Safety Tom put off site a while back, remember?"

"I know, I know. I only meant to go for couple of pints but ended up having a couple of gallons instead in some club in Ilford, top shelf as well. I went back with some quare one to her gaff. I'll never get sense" said Dónal, feeling sorry for himself, but laughing at the same time.

"All I'm saying is watch yourself. That RE used to drink like a fish. I knew him when he was boozing years ago and he was no saint. Now he's the first one to come down on a man for it."

"Sure isn't that always the way – there's none so pure as a reformed hoor!"

They were laughing as they reached the face,

"Now. Have a look in there Dónal" The Badger said, "what do you make of it?"

Dónal took the torch and shone the light into the chamber ahead.

"Give us a push and I'll see what I see" he said as he squirmed into the small opening. Even though he drank a lot he was quite thin. Thin and wiry.

He dragged himself into the hole while The Badger pushed him through from behind. First his head, then his shoulders, broke free from the opening. He felt solid concrete about two feet below and he crawled onto it. He stood up and found his torch by the light from the tunnel behind.

"Are you all right?" He heard The Badger say.

"I'm OK" he said as he switched on his torch. "It looks like I'm in a cellar of some sort."

Dónal shone the light all about. He was in an underground bunker or cellar. The roof of the chamber had collapsed. He could stand upright in the corner where he was but the bulk of the ceiling or roof had fallen in. The air was stale and damp. In front of him was the rubble from the collapsed roof.

"Bomb damage" he thought, "maybe that's why there was no record. But at this depth?"

The Site Investigation hadn't shown anything "London clay all the way", as he had said. But it was nothing new to find an anomaly underground. Soils could change from soft clay to rock within a drive – it all depended on the geology. Or they might come upon a sewer or a water main. His company had made serious money from meeting such unforeseen ground conditions.

As an Engineer, Doral's training was to complete a project safely and on time. All too often Fallon had told him that that wasn't enough – "No Claim No Gain" might have been the company motto.

"Well", Dónal said to himself, "we have a cast iron claim now, no doubt about it – Fallon will be happy!"

"It looks like they'll have to go back to the drawing board. They'll maybe have to find another route for their service tunnel. I'm coming out once I've taken a few photos" he said to the others.

He took out his iPhone and switched it to Camera. Then he took his measuring tape and extended it to the one metre mark. He placed the tape on the floor in front of the spoil heap to lend scale and, standing at the spot where he had entered the cellar, he took a series of photographs, sweeping from left to right in an arc that ensured he had a photographic record of the chamber in the "as found" condition.

On bending down to retrieve the tape, his eye was drawn to a piece of timber protruding from the spoil heap. It was only sticking out an inch or so but it was out of place amongst the dust and rubble.

More by instinct than by any design, he reached down to grab it and pull it away from the rubble. But it wasn't just a piece of loose timber as he had thought. It was solid. He cleared away the spoil around it with his foot, revealing as he did so that the protruding piece of timber was in fact the corner of a small crate.

Using his hands he shoved the covering heap of rubble away from above and about the crate until he could see that there was not one, but three, small wooden boxes, complete with rope handles, sitting in what would once have been the middle of the chamber. He tried to lift one of the crates but it was too heavy and the rotten rope handle gave way.

He went back to the entrance to the chamber.

"Pass me in a nailbar and a trowel Tony" he said to The Badger "I'm after finding something funny down here."

"Are you all right Dónal?" said The Badger as he handed in the tools "do you want me to send wee Jimmy in along with you?"

"No I'm ok but get the lads to set up the grouting stuff – we'll not be building any rings this shift, nor the next one I'd say" said Dónal and, almost in a whisper "keep an ear out for the Resident Engineer – That bollox of an RE will lose his rag if he finds me in here in a confined space on my own. And fire up the jigger every so often like you were working away as normal. They'll wonder topside if they don't hear you making a racket. I'll flash my torch when I want you."

The sound of the Hauser was fearful in the chamber. How those guys put up with it for ten hours a day, every day, was beyond him. That and the heat and the damp and the dust. And the back-breaking work. Bent down from the waist, for four hours or more at a time, squeezed into a four foot hole, drilling and shovelling non-stop! Often in compressed air, under unbearable conditions, to hold the water back in the face!

No amount of money would pay him to do it. No amount! He was challenged by The Badger one time to spend a day at the face after he had said the work wasn't as hard as they made out. He rose to the challenge and spent a shift shovelling behind him. Dónal was fit enough at the time and younger than Phil was now but he only just got through the day. He didn't admit it but it had nearly killed him. He was in no hurry to repeat the experience.

Using the trowel he shoved aside the spoil covering the uppermost box. There was some writing stamped on the lid. It was a series of letters and numbers. He reckoned it was a file reference or some such. Taking up the nailbar he prised away the lid. Inside each box were three ingots, bars, of metal. It looked like gold or brass it was so shiny. The yellow brightness of the metal was reflected in the beam of his torch. He picked up one of the bars. It must have weighed 10kilos or more. There were marks, hallmarks of some kind stamped into the bars. It must be gold. It could only be such. No doubt about it. He had seen smaller such in the Gold Souk in Abu Dhabi. They had had similar marks.

Although he was alone, Dónal looked around, guiltily. Suspicious, greedy even, almost by instinct, in the presence of all that treasure. It was like something out of a movie. He thought of *The Count of Monte Cristo*.

How often did you see guys in films breaking into vaults or banks to get their hands on gold bullion and here he was, sitting on 9 – maybe more – bars of gold at God knows how much an ounce. He lifted one of the bars and tested its weight again. It was as heavy as lead. He scratched the surface to make sure it wasn't in fact lead painted yellow. It wasn't. He was confused, excited.

"Was it really gold? How pure was it? Would there be a reward? Could he keep it? What is gold worth?" he asked himself.

All these questions were racing through Danny's mind when he heard The Badger whispering.

"Are you OK in there? Dónal, Dónal, are you all right?"

"I'm fine Tony. I'm fine. Listen," he whispered through the hole, thinking as he spoke and functioning on pure adrenalin, "shout up for Jimmy. Tell him to bring in the skip and a bundle of empty sandbags."

"I'm going to put some stuff into the bags and pass them out to you, one at a time. Put them in the skip and throw some muck over them".

"What's in there? What did you find Dónal?"

"I'm not certain" he said in the faintest whisper. He knew how sound travelled along a tunnel. How often had he heard the lads at the face bitching about things, often himself, "but I think we're after hitting the jackpot. There are boxes full of gold bars in here."

"Yeah, and pigs might fly. Stop acting the gom. What's in there really?" came the reply.

"Keep your voice down Tony. I'm serious. It might be nothing but I reckon we're onto something here. As *Gaeilge* if that RE comes down." The lads were all fluent in Irish and often used it to keep a secret secret. "He's at a meeting now so we should be OK for an hour or so at least."

While he waited for the skip Dónal moved the bars, one at a time, out of the boxes and over towards the opening. He stacked the nine ingots one on top of the other. He still couldn't get over how heavy each bar was.

Dónal could hear whispering outside. Phil was back at the face.

"Dónal, Dónal" Phil whispered, "can you hear me? I'm shoving the bags through".

The light was blocked out as Phil pushed the empty bags into the cellar.

"I've got them" Dónal replied, "I'm going to put the bars into the bags and give them to you, one at a time. Don't put them into the skip. They'll be too heavy to push and even if you use the winch and pull it into the shaft that bollox of a crane driver will twig the extra weight when he goes to lift it out. The best thing to do for now is to lay them alongside the rails, underneath the hoses and air bagging.

We'll get them topside one at a time later on. Whatever you say, say nothing. Keep this to ourselves for now. That Billy can't keep his mouth shut and God knows what that young fellow out there might do or say if he gets wind of what we have."

Dónal worked fast. He was sweating like a pig, beads of the stuff dripping off his forehead and into his eyes. Whether it was from nerves or excitement or the heat and stale air he couldn't say. His hands were shaking.

"Jesus" he said to himself, "I shouldn't have had all that beer last night."

One by one he bagged up the bars, lifted them and fed them through.

"There's some weight in them" The Badger said "it's like dragging for salmon in Annagry."

"You must have very fat salmon in Donegal" Dónal replied. He stopped as he felt himself getting sick. Like every serious boozer, he had experienced empty retching many a time but now was not the time to weaken.

"Hold" he told himself, "hold, hold, hold" as wave after wave of nausea passed over him. He held onto the edge of the hole and grimaced. The nausea passed.

"Here, coming through again" he said. He passed the bags through until all nine bars were moved out of the cellar. He looked around him. His mind was racing. He had to make the place look as it was before he entered the chamber. The boxes were clearly visible so, using the nailbar, he broke them into smaller pieces and fed them through after the bags.

"Lose them timbers" he whispered.

"Break off the air hose and pass the bagging through" he continued. The Badger passed the hose in. Dónal lay down on his stomach and shoved himself, feet first, back into the hole, pushing himself off the chamber floor.

"Give us a pull Tony" he said and The Badger dragged him by the feet, back towards the tunnel. When only his head and arms were left sticking out he told The Badger to stop. He looked around him, holding the torchlight in his mouth he swept the room again. The only signs he had been in there were his footprints on the dust covered floor. He freed the valve on the hose, causing a powerful flow of air from the compressor to enter the chamber with a rush. His ears popped as he directed the airflow around and about the floor of the chamber, causing the dust within to rise.

He continued this action for a long as he could stick it. The dust was everywhere and he couldn't breathe. He felt another wave of nausea and he could taste the puke in his gullet and in his mouth but he held on until he couldn't see the floor for dust. He switched over the valve.

"Pull me back" he croaked, "Pull me back."

The Badger and Phil dragged Dónal into the tunnel shield. He was coughing and spluttering and cursing.

"Fuck me, fuck me, fuck me" he said as he turned away from the lads and puked. It dawned on him that he had asked the lads for an extra ring and here he was puking one up! There was a joke in there somewhere and he laughed and gagged at the same time.

Phil passed him the bottle of water. He poured some into his mouth, swirled and spat. Then he took a long draft of the liquid. He poured the rest over his head, scraping his knuckles against the roof of the tunnel shield as he did so.

"Fuck it," he grimaced, "fuck this for a game of cowboys."

Then he started to laugh – probably from nerves, but he couldn't help himself. The others looked on and started laughing too. Their laughter rang all the way back to the shaft, distracting Billy Halloran from the Racing Post and causing Jimmy to shout "are ye all right in there?"

The boys laughed even louder when they heard Jimmy.

"Are you alright there Dónal, are you alright?" Jimmy asked again.

"Are you right there Michael, are you right" sang Phil to echo Jimmy and they burst out laughing again.

"I'm weak" Dónal said, "I'm weak. Stop laughing, stop laughing."

"Come on" The Badger said "we'll get this fellow a bit of fresh air before he caves the whole lot in on top of us. He'll be the cause of an earthquake."

The three men crept along the tunnel towards the shaft, passing the bags containing their loot as they went, trying not to laugh. They had the hysteria nearly under control when Dónal started to sing :

"Oh Mary this London's a wonderful sight, there's gangs of men working by day and by night. They don't sow potatoes, nor barley, nor wheat" and the others joined in at that point with "but there's gangs of them digging for gold in the street."

They could hardly stand from laughing as they entered the shaft.

"The three stooges" Billy said to Wee Jimmy "fools laughing at their own ignorance."

"Right, get a grip now" Dónal said "I have to put things in motion and we have to think this thing through. Meanwhile, remember, whatever you say, say nothing."

Dónal was thinking out loud. "First off," he said, in a whisper, "I'm going to tell Fallon we're definitely stuck below and that we'll get a claim out of it. That'll keep him off our backs. Then I'll report the cellar to the site agent. He'll want the Resident Engineer to have a look at it. Remember, as far as everyone is concerned you broke into it to see what it was. That's it. End of. Don't be cheeky. We'd all love to tell Fallon where to stick his job but we can't do that until we've got the stuff out of the tunnel. If we got chased now we would never get back down below so play cagey boys, play cagey! For now, act like nothing out of the ordinary has happened. Get the story straight Tony. You hit a wall down below and broke through it without thinking. Act stupid and play dumb."

"They'll ask you whether you looked into the hole. You say you did but couldn't see anything. All you know is you broke into a chamber of some sort. Say it is like a storm overflow or some such if you're asked." he added.

"I don't know how much that stuff is worth lads but if it is the real thing and I reckon it is, each of them bars is worth a small fortune. They must weigh about 10 Kilos or more each. We'll divide it between the three of us equally. Agreed?"

"Aye, agreed" the others replied and they ascended the ladder in silence as the reality of the find entered into and took hold of their private thoughts.

Chapter Two

A Cover Up

Before anything could be done, Dónal had to square things on the job. He walked along Bishopsgate, pacing off the 30m length of the tunnel from the shaft. It was only an approximation but he reckoned the cellar was underneath a bank, Credit Suisse. The building had been refurbished some years ago – the façade was modern though not new. The marble cladding gave away its age as the more recent trend was for metal and glass. Also, the building looked as if it had been squeezed into a corner at a bend in the street. It would have been wedge-shaped if seen from above. He would check it out on the map later but his instinct told him the bank had been built from scratch on what might have been a bomb site. The buildings all around were banks as well but they were all of the more solid nineteenth century type. All stone faced with heavily ornamented doors and windows. The Bank of England itself was only around the corner in Threadneedle Street.

Credit Suisse looked to be the only new building in the vicinity.

"Had it been constructed above the cellar where they found the gold?" Dónal wondered. "It's possible, very possible" he said to himself in answer.

There weren't any building regulations in place after the war. In the urgency to rebuild not much heed was paid to site surveys as such – it was demolish and rebuild and don't hang around asking questions. There were many bodies unaccounted for in The Blitz and he had heard stories of workers coming across skeletal remains when digging sewer lines and such all over the East End and in The City.

Standing on the street opposite the bank, he took out his notebook and made a sketch. The sketch showed the layout of the street. He marked the position of the tunnel shield below with a "G", for Gold!

That done he headed for the main contractor's site compound where his van was parked. He used the van as his office and sat into it and started writing up his records. He hated that part of the job. The site diary was meant to be completed every day and allocation sheets submitted daily to the contractor also but he often left things go for a week or more, frequently writing them up in the pub on Sunday mornings.

The entries were routine – daily progress was recorded, as was daily activity. In a job like this it was a case of "same old, same old" every day but it was important that diaries were kept up to date as his records would be demanded and examined once he notified the contractor of the stoppage. He couldn't very well lodge a claim for loss of production without having first recorded and established a norm.

Next, he switched on his mobile phone and called Fallon. Fallon was abroad. Dónal could tell from the ringing tone. Kingdom Tunnelling had some work in Abu Dhabi. "Fallon is over there" Dónal thought " he must have got that Mussaffah job. He would only go out there if the contract was to be signed. Corbett is most likely out there as well."

"Where were you?" Fallon said on answering, no "hello" or any such pleasantry, "I'm trying you since before seven, how long before you're out of there? We're losing hand over fist on that job."

"It'll be a while yet" said Dónal "that's why I'm ringing you. The lads are after hitting something down below. Something unforeseen."

Dónal knew Fallon would light on the term. He could see Fallon's face, his eyes narrowing at the thought of the extra profit.

"They're after coming onto a cellar" he continued "they opened it up enough for me to get in. I've photos taken. No one knows about it yet. I'm just going in to the site office now to let them know we're stopped while awaiting instructions. We'll catch up on the grouting today but there'll be no mining until it's sorted out."

"Did you check the boreholes?"

"Of course I did. London Clay all the way. I've told the gang they'll be on dayworks until they get the go ahead. The miners aren't happy with that – they're not making money when they're not building rings and there's only a day at the grouting. I don't want to lose them but they'll fuck off if we don't give them a better dayworks rate. We have a cast iron claim here but we have to keep the lads on board. The Resident Engineer knows them all by sight now and he'll do a headcount every day, mark my words. If we want the claim to get anywhere we have to keep the crew and all the gear together on site full time for the duration."

"Make sure your records are up to date and in order. Take plenty of photos. That nancy boy of a clerk of works called up the office yesterday. He said you were nowhere to be seen and he needed you to sign for some delivery or other. Were you on the beer or what?"

"Don't mind that wanker – he's only angling for a drink himself. I wouldn't give him the steam off my piss. Mind you, he'd probably like it if I did! I signed the docket this morning – it was for some bentonite I got them to hold in stock for us. He's a proper bollox."

"Right then, you write to BGW. Tell them you're stopped. I'll get Gordon to go down there – he'll put the thing together."

Dónal didn't like the sound of that. He didn't need anybody else mooching around the place while he sorted things out.

"Keep Gordon where he is. The RE can't stand him. I'll handle the claim. Gordon can do the measure from the office. I'll send him the records. The RE told me never to let Gordon near him again since that time he laid siege to him in Chester last year. Gordon was trying to get him to sign the Completion Certificate before he'd even inspected the work. He really pissed him off that time – keep Gordon out of it if you want the RE to play ball! You would be better off coming down yourself. You could bring him out for a meal and keep him sweet."

"No can do, not until late next week. I'll be out of the country."

With that Fallon hung up. Dónal looked at the phone "ignorant bollox" he said to himself out loud as he laughed. He had bought some time though. Not much, but it would be enough.

Dónal reached into the back of the van for the Site Memo book. He drafted a memo, addressed to BGW. In the memo he formally advised BGW that Kingdom Tunnelling Ltd. had, in the course of its work, encountered an unforeseen obstruction and was now stopped while awaiting an instruction from BGW. Short and sweet!

Dónal knew that this little note would not please BGW's Site Manager at first as it signalled a claim in the offing. However, once the claim was seen to be viable BGW would row in on Kingdom's side. BGW and Kingdom would then raise a joint claim against the Client. Ultimately, the cost of the claim would be borne by the City of London and/or its insurers. While all this was being argued, Dónal and the boys could shift the gold. Then they could figure out what to do with it.

He broke into a sweat when he thought of the gold again. He had put it to the back of his mind since leaving Credit Suisse but now it was firmly back in pole position.

"Jesus Dónal" he said to himself "how're you going to sort this one out?"

He walked over to the steps leading to BGW's offices. The site secretary, Angie, was standing at the top of the steps, smoking a cigarette.

"Here's trouble" she smiled as Dónal climbed the up steps towards her "another "please be advised note" I suppose?"

"It's a thing of nothing babe, just another one of my famous memos."

"Oi, don't you "babe" me I'm not your babe, I'm not anybody's babe!"

"Gorgeous then?"

"I'm not anybody's "gorgeous" either."

"You could be mine if you wanted to be."

"In your dreams Dónal Boy, in your dreams."

"Hey, don't knock it till you've tried it. We should go out for a drink and a bite to eat some night. I'll put it on expenses and tell Fallon I brought you out on account of you did some typing for me."

"Oh Yeah? I don't think your Mr. Fallon is that generous."

"He's not. But he will think it's to his advantage to have you on our side."

"Yeah right! As if!"

Angela and Dónal had known one another off and on since Kingdom first did some work for BGW up North. She liked him. She liked his attitude, his disregard for convention, his sense of humour. And he wasn't bad looking. Not great looking but not bad. She knew he was a bit wild though. And he had a bit of a reputation where women were concerned.

Still, he made her laugh. He didn't take himself too seriously, unlike most of the blokes she knew. Even the memos he wrote were funny, written very much tongue-in-cheek. Made all the funnier because the recipients seldom or never realized he was taking the piss out of them.

And Dónal had always liked Angela. She was a very attractive girl, petite and sexy, even in the unflattering business suits she wore to work. He reckoned she would be worth seeing in a swimsuit or, even better, in her underwear, or better again, wearing shag-all!

"Yeah right, as if" he mimicked her Scottish lilt. Then he said "seriously Angie, I meant it. Would you like to go out with me, on Friday? It doesn't have to be a big deal. I like you. I've always liked you. What have you got to lose?" He surprised himself as he said it. The words just sort of tripped out. He even reddened a little.

Angela looked at Dónal again. She sensed he was for real. She saw he had somehow revealed something personal, something private about himself. He did like her, she was pretty sure of that. It never dawned on her that there could be more than banter between them though.

"Why Mr. Dónal, I do believe you're blushing. All right then" she said, without thinking, "I'll go out for a drink with you. But not in Ilford!"

"I don't live in Ilford" Dónal said, "I'm renting a gaff in Southend, near the seafront. We did a job in the airport there before starting this one. I kept on the apartment when this contract came up. What makes you think I live in Ilford?"

"Oh, just something a wee birdie told me."

Dónal wondered who had spotted him in Ilford last night. He made a mental note that he must have been of some interest to her if his whereabouts were being talked of though.

"Well that wee birdie is singing out of tune. Southend is a dump though. I'll not bring you there! Where do you live? I'll pick you up and we can go on somewhere."

"Billericay, near the railway station" Angie said, writing the address down for him.

"I'll find it, I've got Satnav. Now, sign for receipt of the memo here please babe, sorry, sexpot." She raised an eyebrow at that and laughed.

"Ha. I was right, it is another "please be advised" memo" she said. "At least you're consistent."

"Until Friday then, Gorbals."

"Not Gorbals, Pollokshaws" she replied "can youse not tell from the way I speak? We talk posh Scots in Pollokshaws."

"No such thing as "posh" in Glasgow. Maybe in Edinburgh, but Glasgie – no way".

The Site Manager, Andy Wall, stuck his head out of his office.

"Ang", he said "I need you take some minutes. Kick that reprobate out before he lodges yet another claim."

"Too late Andy" Dónal heard her say as he slipped out while she handed him the memo "it's a "please be advised"one."

Dónal walked down the steps. He was smiling as he walked. Not smirking like earlier when he thought about the gold but smiling a genuine, happy smile. Until that moment he hadn't realized just how much he liked her.

"Fuck it Dónal", he said to himself, "you've hit the jackpot today. Your luck is in." With that he walked over to the bookies and backed the horse numbered twelve, the number of Angela's house in Billericay, in the race about to go off. He didn't even check out the horse's form but he put a pony each way on it at eights. It came nowhere.

"Can't have it all" he said as he tore up the betting slip "I've got the girl, I've got the gold" he sang in his head to the tune of the old Rolling Stones" number "You've Got The Silver" as he walked back to the shaft.

"Stick around until about four lads" he said "then you can head away."

He called The Badger aside. "Leave that yellow stuff where it is for now. Drop off the lads and I'll see you and Phil in The Angel around six – we have a few things to figure out. I think I have a plan but it'll need to be thought through. I'll have to stick around for an hour or so in case the Resident Engineer wants a pow-wow but I'll know where we're going immediately afterwards."

Dónal sat back into the van. His hangover had passed and he didn't feel the need for a drink any longer. Nor did he want one. There was a coke bottle laced with vodka in the glove compartment. He kept it there for emergencies, that is to say, for those early morning hours when the pubs were closed and he needed a cure. It was a trick he had picked up when working in the Middle East. But he had neither need nor desire for alcohol. It was weird. His priorities had changed.

"I'll deal with the gold, I'll deal with the lads, I'll deal with Fallon, I'll deal with Corbett and I'll deal with the RE" he thought "no bother! I'll box them off one at a time and sort the lot out. But Angela? What was that about? She's a beauty! Why the fuck did she say she'd go out with him? Why the fuck did he ask her? He'll mess it up. This can't be a one night stand! He didn't want it to be one but it might end up that way. She might like him as a diversion at work but any other way? She would hardly want to start something, and, even if they did get it together, now, with all that's going on, it would be stupid, if not insane, but he did really like the girl."

Then it dawned on him. It dawned on him that he hadn't felt this way about any woman in an age. It dawned on him that this was more than a fancy. It hit him that he was maybe in love with her and that he had been in love with her for some time, maybe even since she used to give him a big friendly wave as she drove past him in the marshalling yard in that job in Preston. They didn't have much direct contact then but when they met the following year in Cumbria, he remembered how his heart lifted on seeing her. She was friendly and pretty and normal. And she liked him. Her eyes said so. And he liked her. Oh, yes, he bloody well did like her. He just hadn't twigged how much. He had wanted her then though he didn't either admit it or allow it because she was simply too nice for him. His women tended to get hurt and she didn't need a raggle taggle gypsy-oh screwing things up for her.

And they had to work together. It was a cardinal rule of his not to get involved with any bit of stuff he had to work with but he wanted her. He wanted her now and he would if he could put the world and its worries on hold until they got it together. And if she was to be a challenge then it would be a welcome one.

"Roll on Friday" he said in his own mind.

Dónal hung around until Andy rang him after his meeting with the RE. "You're to stand the crew down until the RE prepares a report on the chamber below, Dónal, and you're to keep the crew on site to assist as requested. Make sure all is shipshape and everything squared away. We can expect the bigwigs. The RE has referred the whole thing to The Consulting Engineer for review and a redesign. It might be a reroute."

"They won't go for a reroute Andy. They should let us fill that chamber with grout and we'd go through it no bother ", Dónal replied.

"You know that and I know that and we both know they'll come to that conclusion in the end but they have hoops to jump through before they get there. It's the way of things. As well you know. Meanwhile sit tight."

"Will you send me an instruction so? Today, please if possible. Fallon and Corbett are giving me grief. They want to send Gordon down but if we're stopped through no fault of mine they'll leave me be I reckon. I know Fallon has something lined up for me abroad."

"No worries there. I'll tell Fallon you're to stay on site until further notice and I don't want that nuisance Gordon around anymore than you do. Why Corbett holds on to him is beyond me! I'll draft the memo now for Angela to type. That'll give you an excuse to chat her up when you collect it."

"Me! Chat Angie up? No way. You're mistaking me for another surely?"

"Piss off Dónal, I have work to do. Just for once I wish you guys would come on site, do the job and fuck off like everybody else. And leave my secretary alone!"

The Badger and Phil were in The Angel before Dónal. Quite a while before him, judging by the state of the table they were sat at.

"How's about you Dónal? What are you having? The Guinness is not bad here" said Phil as Dónal sat down beside him.

"No such thing as bad porter as far as I am concerned, only some porter is better than others. And the best porter of all is free porter! I'll try a pint then, just to see what it's like, like."

The Badger and Dónal waited until Phil returned to the table with three pints.

"Well" said Phil "how did you get on?"

Dónal lifted his glass and downed a good half pint. "Christ but I needed that" he said. "Right", he went on, "I met the RE and the Site Agent. They've accepted we have a claim for an unforeseen condition at the face and they asked me for our proposal for finishing the drive. I went around in circles and gave them some options – I said we could complete the work by cutting out the obstruction and mining around it by means of timber heading. Or, I said, we could abandon the drive and they could redesign the whole thing and give us another route. As I knew well, either of these solutions would result in long delayed completion dates and huge extra costs. They did a lot of tut-tutting and headshaking."

"Then," I said to them, "the only other way forward might be for the Resident Engineer to allow us to fill the chamber below with foam concrete or grout. Then we can burrow through the external wall and that part of the grouted chamber on the line of the tunnel."

"What did they say to that?"

"They did some more humming and hawing and asked a few questions, mainly in regard to how long it will take but I reckon they will go along with the idea. We should know tomorrow but I'm certain that we'll be told to complete the tunnel and that means we retain control over those bars of chocolate down below."

"Good man Dónal, good man. Now, what are we going to do with those bars of chocolate, as you call them?"

"We can't just sell them on the open market. That much I know. I don't know anyone who might be able to offload the stuff. I know a few guys who buy and sell waccy baccy and I know a scouser in Southampton who is dodgy but this is way, way out of their league. You guys probably know someone in Donegal with an IRA connection but I'm not dealing with those guys. We would all end up on the side of a road in Tyrone with a bullet in the head."

"If we could get the stuff out to Abu Dhabi, we'd be able to find a buyer there I reckon. Corbett and Fallon are setting up some work out there. The lads in the yard in Brum are putting a load of gear together to ship out. They wanted to know when our rig would be free. The best thing would be if Fallon sent us out there. I know it's a bollox of a place but if we were to be sent over there we could hide the chocolate bars in the container. The tunnel rig and all the gear weighs tons so the weight of the chocolate wouldn't be noticed. Customs wouldn't be a problem as the gear is leaving the UK and they never check goods coming into Mussaffah from here."

"You might be onto something there Dónal. Phil was just saying the same thing. The stuff is no good if we can't sell it. How much do you reckon it's worth?"

"I'm not sure but that type of stuff is worth over £1,200 per ounce. That's about 18 grand per pound. That means a kilo of the stuff is worth 36,000 quid. And each bar is about 10 kilos. That makes each bar worth £360,000! Our nine bars are worth over four million quid. We're millionaires boys! If we can get shut of the goods, that is".

"For now, I reckon the best thing to do is to sneak it out of that part of the tunnel where it is first thing tomorrow morning. It's too close to the chamber where it is. Move it back along the way nearer the shaft and shove the bars in behind the airline."

"I'll send Halloran away on some job or other and I'll man the crane. We'll lift the stuff out of the hole ourselves. We'll do it while Jimmy is off buying the breakfast stuff. We'll put it in the back of the lock-up, under the pallets of bentonite. No one will look under there."

"We have to stick together on this, lads. No solo runs. If we can get the stuff out to Abu Dhabi I reckon we're home and dry. I know a few shady characters out there who would fall over themselves to get hold of those bars of chocolate."

"I don't know" said The Badger, "as I said to Phil earlier we might be better off handing it in and maybe getting a reward or something. I don't want any trouble. All I know about is pulling muck out of the ground and pulling fish out of the sea. This is serious stuff. We could all end up inside."

"Listen to me", Dónal said, "we're never going to get an opportunity like this again. As long as we stick together and keep our traps shut nothing will go wrong. We're like the three musketeers."

He raised his glass "One For All And All For One" he said as the others joined in. "Now" Dónal said "I must be off home. I'm cutting down on the booze until this is over. I need to keep my head clear. Don't stay out all night – we've things to sort out tomorrow". Phil looked at him, smiled and said "there's none so pure as a reformed hoor".

Chapter Three
ASSET TRANSFERS

Dónal didn't sleep very well that night. He had tried to watch some television but he couldn't settle. He thought of going for a few beers but he held back. One drink would lead to another so he chose to stay in. He went to bed early, well, early for him, at least, at around eleven. He slept for an hour or so but awoke with a start.

"The jigs" he said to himself. It was always like that on the night of the morning after. He would sleep in fits and starts – his head populated by weird dreams when he nodded off and by weird anxieties when awake.

"It's just a chemical" he would say to himself "it will pass." He knew it was part of alcohol withdrawal but all that was going on made it harder to endure than normally. He needed a drink but he resisted the temptation to get up and go to the fridge where he had some beer or to the van where his emergency vodka was.

Instead he took out his laptop and did some research on the internet. First, he checked out the spot where they had found the chocolate. He was right – the junction above the cellar had been obliterated during the war. As had figured the building where Credit Suisse now stood had suffered a direct hit. That building had either been attached to or was part of the huge Bank of England complex in nearby Threadneedle Street.

"Curiouser and curiouser" Dónal said to himself. He followed the connections, lighting on websites where Bullion and Wartime figured but most of these dealt with Nazi Gold and the finds of same.

There was a reference to the transfer of Britain's Gold to Canada during the war. The government of the day had not been very confident in 1939/40 that a German invasion would fail. Secret steps were taken to have the nation's gold reserves transferred across the Atlantic to safer havens in Canada. It was one of the best kept secrets of the war and made for fascinating reading. The Bullion reserves were moved under military escort from The City to Southampton.

Neither the British public nor Britain's ally, America,, was told of this transfer as on the one hand, the news of it might have cause public dismay in Britain and on the other hand, news of it could have caused American distrust of Britain's motive.

The gold bars were placed one at a time into boxes. Each box was sealed and signed for on dispatch from the Bank of England and on arrival at Southampton where every box was checked and receipted. The procedure was repeated when the crates were loaded on board the ships and again at arrival in Halifax before onward dispatch to the Royal Bank of Canada's vaults in Toronto. Not a single ounce of gold had been lost during the entire operation – it was one of the greatest secrets of the war.

"Then" Dónal wondered "if it was all so well controlled and if every bar of gold was accounted for, how come there were nine bars left down below? Unless", he figured, "not all the gold was dispatched as planned. What if someone had held some back? That's the only way those bars could have been left in the chamber. Say some banker wasn't so confident about letting go of the gold on deposit in his bank. Say the gold was never officially even there. It was a Swiss Bank, after all – the Swiss did as much business with Germany as they did with Britain during the war. Say the gold was dodgy in one way or the other? It may have been unrecorded."

"If that was the case" he mused "then it would explain how the gold ended up where it did, unknown to anyone, as, if it never officially existed, then officially it was never lost. Only the Bank Manager and maybe one or two of his staff would have known about it and they may have been killed when the bomb hit Bishopsgate. A lot of ifs and buts and twists and turns certainly, but all entirely possible. Unlikely, but possible!"

The following day, Wednesday, he went along to the shaft as usual. The gang was there ahead of him, hanging around the cabin, drinking mugs of tea and killing time by tidying up the bits and pieces around and about the site. The Badger was stripping down some piece of equipment or other and drying oil off one part with a rag and pouring oil from a can onto another part.

Phil looked the worse for wear –"I see you went home straight afterwards like you said you would." Dónal said to him, laughing.

"Go way from me you" said Phil "If I hadn't had to meet you I wouldn't have had a drop. Not a drop."

"You could have drunk lemonade. I didn't pour them pints down your gullet. Look at me, fresh as a daisy, see. I can control my drink."

Dónal called Billy over. "Billy, will you take my van up to the yard in Solihull later? Tell Alex there's something wrong with the bearings and ask him to give you a jeep for me while he sorts it out. There'll be no need for you here today. Go now before breakfast and come straight back as I want the RE to think we have a full crew on site. Tell Alex I want one of the Toyotas."

"Fuck that I'll miss the grub" Billy whinged."You could do with losing a few pounds" countered Dónal "all day sitting in that crane has left you a stone heavier than you were at the start of the job. Get some scran on the way and get a receipt. I'll cover it."

"Give me the keys so." Billy said, happier now that he would have a free breakfast and a nice easy drive in the van. With that he hopped into the vehicle and disappeared before Dónal could change his mind.

They waited until Jimmy went off to the minimart to get the bits and pieces for the breakfast.

"Right lads you two go down below and move the chocolate bars into the shaft while I get the crane fired up."

Dónal started the old beast up. It had seen better days. Black smoke billowed at first from the exhaust pipes behind, turning to white once he revved the engine a bit *"Habemus Papam"* Dónal smirked. He manoeuvred the crane levers. He could drive most kinds of construction plant but a crane? He released one of the levers gently and the jib dropped slightly. One by one he tickled the controls, hand and foot, until he had the basics figured out. "Nothing to it really" he reckoned after about twenty minutes..

Phil climbed out of the shaft and walked over to Dónal. "The chocolate bars are below on the pit bottom. We've two sitting in the skip below. I'll bank you so watch my signals. Take it handy and you'll be alright. If that idiot Halloran can drive it anyone can."

Phil was right – it wasn't rocket science. On the first lift he overcompensated and the jib drew the skip in against the wall of the shaft. The skip bounced about a bit but Dónal held his nerve and winched the load up and onto the hardstand next the shaft. Phil guided the skip to ground and moved quickly to spirit the sacks into the container. They repeated the operation five times until all nine bars were stashed in the back of the store, out of sight behind the tunnelling gear.

The Badger climbed out of the pit as Dónal shut the crane down.

"That's the first move over in this particular game of cowboys" Dónal said as he jumped down from the crane "and there ain't no sign of any posse on the horizon. Yippee-Ay-Ey – let's head for the chuck wagon."

They were just back in the cabin when wee Jimmy arrived back from the shop with the shopping.

"Here comes the camel, laden with spices and gold from the East" Dónal said without thinking.

"Gold is right" said The Badger and the three burst out laughing.

"Are you guys smoking dope or what?" Jimmy said. "Youse were giggling like a bunch of schoolgirls yesterday as well. You're only out of the hole for half a day. Must be the fresh air and sunlight is gone to your heads. Anyone would think you guys had won the lottery or something. The sooner the jiggers are started up again the better. Then maybe we get back to normal."

"Come on, lads, settle down. Jimmy, start the grub. I have to see the RE in an hour. Give Phil a few extra sausages. He likes them Gold Medal ones" Dónal laughed as he ducked out of the cabin.

Chapter Four

SOUTHAMPTON

Like many a man who works long hours for long periods, idleness did not sit easily with Dónal. He awoke early on Thursday as usual, at six, but he couldn't get back to sleep. He had the same problem when on holidays. Often his body clock was only adjusting to holiday time when he had to return to work. The fact that he had a load of gold sitting unguarded in the lock-up weighed on his mind and didn't help matters.

He thought about paying a visit to BGW's office, more to see Angie than for any particular reason but he decided against it. He might only be drawn into a conversation with Andy who might rethink some aspect of the plan and before he knew it he would end up rejigging things all over again.

More for something to do than for any other reason he headed in to the shaft. The Badger and Phil were there before him.

"I couldn't keep away, couldn't sleep" he said to them.

"Same as that Dónal," Phil replied, "same as that. Sure what else are we to do? We were in the digs and there's only breakfast TV to look at there. We thought of getting a flight over to Derry and spending the weekend at home. We might still do that."

"You're as well off stopping around for now. Later on today when Travis Perkins opens I'll go over and buy new security padlocks for the lock-up. I'll get ones with three keys so we'll have one each. We'll lock it up and keep it locked except when at least one of us is about. I trust you both but in case owt happens we all need access."

"We'll be here for another three weeks. There's no need for us over the weekend strictly speaking but we should keep an eye on things nevertheless."

"Will be doing the grouting, Dónal? Will we get a mining rate for that?" The Badger said.

"Jesus, Tony, you're going to take a million quid out of this and you're worried about a couple of pounds extra per shift! For fucks sake!"

"Old habits die hard Dónal, sorry. Old habits."

"Anyway, we will only be helping out on the grouting. All you will have to do will be to get the hoses into the chamber. We won't have to do any mixing or pumping. I'll have forty tonnes of ready mixed grout pumped into that basement on Monday or Tuesday and that will destroy any evidence.

As soon as the grout is gone off on Thursday say, you lads will complete the tunnel. Then we get ready for Abu Dhabi. Fallon has put me in charge out there so I'll be in control of picking the crews. I'm going to bring Wee Jimmy out with us and I think we should give him a cut out of our bit as he's part of the gang."

"What about Halloran?" The Badger asked.

Both Phil and Dónal looked at him.

"Have you lost the run of yourself?" Dónal said. "Halloran won't be wanted out there as we'll be hiring in cranes and they'll come with drivers. He's not getting a shilling of my money, no way. He'll tell Fallon and we'll all be in the shit."

"Aye, aye. You're right. He's only a bollox. I don't know what I was thinking."

"Park that van up against the lock-up and we'll go and get a civilised breakfast. Then we'll get the padlocks like I said."

They walked towards Liverpool Street and found a big café near The Old Bailey. It was choc-a-bloc with ebony robed lawyers, male and female, and their clients.

"We're moving up in the world already boys" Dónal said as he ordered up three "Rumpole Specials" with extra fried bread all round, "some of these guys are just like us, boys, rich! It's nice to be among our own."

They took their meal at leisure for a change and afterwards Dónal bought the padlocks. They returned to the compound and put the new locks in place. Dónal distributed the six keys.

"Now lads, no one can get at our chocolate but us. Keep the container locked from here on in. If anyone from BGW asks why we're keeping it shut tell them we're missing some tools and we don't want to lose any more. Tell them I said it was to be kept locked at all times from now on. You can head off home now and I'll see you Monday. Leave your mobiles on over the weekend just in case I need to talk to either of you."

He looked up in passing at BGW's offices but there was no sign of her. He thought she might be outside having a cigarette but no such luck.

"Grow up" he said to himself, "you're behaving like a love-sick schoolboy."

With that he called Kingdom's Head Office and sorted out some bits and pieces. He made sure that Halloran had collected the Landcruiser and the other gear they would need. He placed a provisional order for sixty cubic metres plus of non shrink grout along with one hundred metres of delivery hose for the coming Tuesday afternoon.

"Keep everything, do everything, as would be normal until we ship out" he said to himself.

But what he was about to do next was not normal. Not normal for Dónal anyway. It would have been normal for Dónal to spend a gift day off work in a pub, preferably one near a bookie so he could indulge in his preferred vices, drinking and gambling, with maybe some womanising thrown in once the racing was over.

It would have been normal for him to wake up the next day alongside some slapper whose name he couldn't even hazard a guess at no more than figure out whether he had either picked her up or had himself been picked up.

But Dónal did something that was entirely abnormal for him. He went shopping. Shopping for clothes, proper clothes, that is. Clothes other than jeans and t-shirts!

He didn't go overboard though. Saville Row was nearby but he headed back to Southend and went to Marks & Spencer's. He bought half a dozen plain cotton shirts, three white, three blue. Six pairs of boxer shirts and six pairs of socks, wondering in passing why everything came in packs of three and then wondering if anyone else ever wondered the same thing.

He was going to buy a jacket of some sort when his eye fell on a beige linen suit. "Now that's class" he thought. He tried a forty two jacket on for size – it was perfect, a tiny bit too big if anything but he hated tight fitting clothes.

"That'll do me" he said, stuffing the suit into his basket. Then he tried on a couple of pairs of loafers, found his size and headed for the tills and escape. The entire operation took less than fifteen minutes. He hated shopping with a passion. He felt more claustrophobic in a department store than he did in a four foot tunnel if the truth be known but he reckoned Angie was worth the sacrifice.

His shopping finished, Dónal thought he might have a few beers but he didn't really want to do that so, more to kill time than anything else he decided he would take a spin to Southampton where an old friend of his, Mick Barrett, lived. He had no way of knowing it at the time but Barrett was to have a small but significant part in the drama that was later to unfold. Mick didn't drink. He used to one time but not any longer so Dónal knew the pub would not feature in his visit.

Mick was out when he called but his big woman, as Mick called her, told Dónal he was gone to the house in Saint Mary's. Mick was a semi-retired builder with an interest in buying, refurbishing and then selling on near derelict properties in Southampton's inner city area. When Southampton FC moved from its old stadium, The Dell, to the huge complex in Saint Mary's the value of properties soared in both places. In The Dell because the team was moving out and in Saint Mary's because the team was moving in!

"Mick, you old bollox, how goes it?" said Dónal on finding him. He had his head under the bonnet of a van parked outside the house in Saint Mary's Road.

"Well fuck me Dónal. Of all the! How the devil are you? What brings you around here? There's a woman has me haunted for news about you every time I see her. Della."

"Della wot drinks Stella?"

"The same one. Won't look at another man she says. Thinks you're pure sex on legs. Isn't that right Fez?"

"Too bloody right" said Fez from underneath the van. "I tried it on but got the knock back. How you doing Don? Long time no see."

"I'm good boys, I'm good. I had a bit of time to kill so I said I'd shoot down to mushland and see my old muckers."

"You'll set the place alight Dónal. The Oxford is gone to fuck. Same old faces in there every day trying to make the few beers last."

"Tell me about it. I lived that life myself for long enough but guess what? I'm off the beer, well, off the hard stuff anyway!"

"About time" said Mick.

"No way" said Fez.

"True boys. Sad but true. I've got a lot going on just now so I want to keep the head straight."

"Must be a woman Fez. Some bit of stuff has gotten to him at long last."

"Partly right, partly wrong. We'll go over to Maltese Toni's for a cup of tea and I'll fill you in."

"Tea, tea?" Fez said. "Sub me a tenner, Mick I'm going for a pint."

Dónal gave Fez a score "Have two pints Fez, have two!"

Fez went across the road while the others headed for the caff. They ordered two teas from Tony and they shot the breeze for a while talking about nothing in particular.

Dónal didn't mention the chocolate but he told Mick of the upcoming trip to The Emirates. Dónal wanted to tell Mick the full story. He trusted Mick without question. Mick had been like a father to him but he didn't need to know about things that didn't concern him. Also, telling Mick would break the bond with the others.

"You should talk to Gian before you go out there this time. Himself and myself are joint owners of a small development in Hayling Island. The second finish is complete and I'm going out there now. You should come along. Gian's brother has a rake of men working for him in Dubai and in some other place out there. He's in a big way – he ships in the labour from India and subs out the work. Like Murphy did here years ago. Gian's brother is one of the richest men in Punjab Province. And one of the trickiest, if he's anything like Gian. Saki is his name."

They headed out to Hayling Island, Dónal squashed into the passenger seat of Mick's tiny van alongside tool boxes and batteries and a half ladder.

"Guy is loaded yet he could be mistaken for a pauper, covered from head to toe in plaster dust" Dónal thought, "may some things never change!"

Gian was there before them, standing by a brand new Merc. Almost showing it off.

He put his hand out to Dónal and Dónal shook it warmly.

"Mr. Engineer Mr. Engineer Dónal" Gian said "Barrett bring you along to measure me up eh, measure me up yes?"

"It would take a better man than me to get the measure of you Gian. Guddah and how're you keeping?"

"Guddah, Guddah, I'm wery vell, wery vell indeed."

Dónal had forgotten how Gian repeated himself all the time. And his pronunciation!

Gian & Mick left Dónal by the vehicles while they walked over to the building site. Their discussions were private and in any event were of little interest to Dónal.

They were only gone twenty minutes or so when they returned. They were both in a good mood. Mick had a very roguish, boyish, way about him and it was more evident than normal.

"Easy to see you guys pulled a stroke of some sort" Dónal said as they came towards him, beaming with laughter.

"You could say that Mr Engineer Dónal, you could say that" said Gian. "Mick say you going back to Dubai, back to Dubai?"

"Well, Abu Dhabi this time but near enough."

"No matter, no matter" he said as he rooted in his wallet.

"Ha I know I have it, I know I have it. Here, Take it, take it" Gian said as he gave Dónal a business card.

"This is my brother Saki's telephone numbers in Dubai and in India see in Dubai and in India. I vill call him and tell him to get good vorkers for you. Good vorkers. Only Sikhs mind, only Sikhs from Punjab. Best of vorkers, best of vorkers."

Dónal took the card from him and thanked him. He put the card into his wallet and thought no more of it as they returned to Southampton. But he was to make use of the card, later, in Abu Dhabi. And he was to be glad, wery glad of it then.

Dónal and Mick went back to Saint Mary's Road where Dónal had left his car. They had a quick bite to eat in Toni's. Burger and chips and heavy on the ketchup before Dónal drove back to Southend. For the first time in years he went to bed early and fell asleep on hitting the pillow. He slept an untroubled sleep, dream free and nightmare free and sweat free and when he awoke, he awoke fully refreshed and ready for operation Angie.

Chapter Five

ANGIE

While Dónal was gallivanting around the country and setting things up for the coming week, Angie was at work as normal, even though she was more than a bit distracted. She was looking forward to Friday night if a little apprehensive. She asked Andy for an early finish on the coming Friday. She'd booked an appointment at a hairdresser's she told him. She didn't mention she had also booked a session on the sunbed to be followed by a facial.

"I knew it" Andy said "you're going out with that shamrock smoothy, Dónal."

"No way" she protested "I wouldn't be seen dead with that guy. What makes you think I would anyway? A lassie would want tae be desperate."

"Angie" Andy said to her, "I'm only on my third marriage and I've only got four daughters. Don't you think I don't know the signs?"

"What signs?"

"Angie, any fool can see there's something between you two. He makes you laugh for one and he's forever popping in and out of here. I reckon he sends me at least three notes a day just so he gets a chance to chat to you."

"Never, you're out of your head. No way. We just have a laugh now and then the odd time he comes in."

"If you say so Ang, if you say so. Don't get me wrong, I like the guy. He's a bit wild but he's OK is our Dónal. I just don't want to see you get hurt pet."

"Don't worry, we're just going out for a drink."

"Ha, I knew it! I spotted it ages ago. I knew there was a spark between you when we were in Solihull. Took you long enough to get it together. Be good and be careful. You hear me?"

"Yeah, yeah! I hear you, I hear you."

"Go on then" Andy said "and you might as well take the whole day off on Friday, I'll book you in but you owe me. You'll need the full day anyway to beautify yourself for the Dónal fellow. He's one lucky boy though. One lucky boy."

"Wiseass, full day indeed, but thanks and I did listen to you."

And Angela had listened to Andy. She always did. She knew Andy cared about her and she trusted him. He was like an uncle to her. Like an uncle and a father and a brother.

There was indeed, as Dónal had sensed, a huge vacuum in her life.

Angela's father had been a well known Glasgow firebrand of The Left. A skilled worker in stained glass, he resented the fact that he depended on the Glasgow Churches and Kirks for his income. He would work all week and spend all weekend in the pubs, rolling home singing snatches of "The Red Flag" and declaring to all and sundry that Ramsay MacDonald was a traitor.

Angela's mom put up with it for years for the sake of Angie until the day she died. The police came to the door late one evening. Angie was eight at the time. Her father was asleep on the couch. They woke him up and one of the policemen threw water in his face to sober him up a bit. They had just pulled the body of a woman out of the Clyde. The social services card belonged to a woman residing at their address.

A policewoman stayed with her while her dad went to identify the body. A verdict of accidental death was recorded but the dogs in the street knew she had taken her own life and her reason for so doing.

Her father tried to look after her. He quit drinking but went into a deep depression.

He would spend all day every day sat in a chair wrapped in a blanket, crying, just crying.

The neighbours tried to help at first but eventually Social Services took over and she was put into care. She remained in care until her sixteenth birthday. Her father had died when she was in a foster home but she refused to attend his funeral.

The only good thing her father had done through all his years working and drinking was to maintain payments into a Trade Union Insurance scheme. When Angela left State

Care at seventeen she had enough money to pay for a secretarial course. So it was she ended up working for BGW. First in Dumfries, where Andy took her under his wing and later, on various contracts throughout the country. She felt safe with Andy and he always made space for her in his set-up.

She had had relationships but had yet to meet a man that really touched her inner being. She didn't analyse things but the fact of the matter is that she had issues with trust. Andy was like the father she never really had and it was nice to know he looked out for her. He was in many ways her best friend.

But he was wrong about Dónal. She was sure of that, she was sure of Dónal. She felt it in her soul, in her very being. She felt it when he smiled at her. She felt when he waved at her from the yard below. But most of all she felt it when he looked at her with those all telling, all knowing eyes.

He couldn't hide it. His eyes betrayed him every time. It was like he was able to reveal his own soul while at the same time looking into hers so that she felt compelled to fix and hold his eyes in hers for an instant and in that instant when his blue eyes captured fully her green ones, nothing but nothing else in God's universe mattered to her and she could tell he felt the same something, the same way, in that weird, wonderfully weird moment.

"Oh God" she said to herself, then, unknowingly echoing Dónal said "roll on Friday!"

Chapter Six

A NIGHT OUT

Before Dónal left Southend to pick Angela up he popped into a florist and picked up a small mixed bunch of fresh cut flowers. Nothing ostentatious but a far remove from the standard filling station offerings that he always reckoned were the cheapskate philanderer's dead giveaway.

Thus suited and booted and bringing his offering he rang the doorbell to Angela's house in Billericay. The door was answered by a pretty young thing wearing a nurse's uniform and sporting a badge stating her name and status.

"Are those for me"? she said. "I'm Mary Anne by the way".

"Your lover boy doughnut is here Ang" she shouted up the stairs "he's all right so he is. Better than you said".

"I'm glad you approve, meringue" Dónal said laughing.

"You never said he was a smart ass Ang. Watch this one. I'm off. See you tomorrow and don't do anything I wouldn't do."

"There's nothing you wouldn't do" Angie said, "absolutely nothing."

With that Mary Ann left, leaving Dónal standing in the hallway with the flowers in his hand. He found the kitchen and was looking for a vase or something when he looked to find she had come down stairs and was standing in the doorway.

"Wow" Dónal gasped, "wow, you look stunning. Stunning and fantastic and gorgeous and magnificent and just simply too beautiful to be true. Wow!"

She was wearing a simple yet elegant plain dress of the deepest truest emerald green he had ever seen. No frills or ruffs, just a tiny belt around her tiny waist. It was short but not too short and it covered her shapely tanned legs to just above the knee.

There were half sleeves on the dress and on her left hand she wore a simple gold torque.

Around her neck was a plain gold filigree chain and she sported tiny, matching earrings.

She smelt of heaven and vanilla and a hundred thousand allures from the bazaars of furthest Samarkand yet her scent didn't overpower.

"Steady on" Angie said "this is just the way I look when I'm not in the office."

"Then you shouldn't come in any more – not", he backtracked "that you don't look gorgeous every day. But this evening, I'm lost for words, pet, lost for words."

"That'd be a first then!"

"I'm serious Angie. You look fantastic, really fantastic."

"Thanks" she smiled. "You don't scrub up too bad yourself Mister Dónal. I reckon you'll do. Are we going out or what?"

"Yes, we're going out though I wouldn't mind staying in with just you on the menu."

"Get off! Don't be so bloody corny. Where are you taking me?"

"Remember you said you loved Portugal one day. We were talking about holidays?"

"Vaguely, but I do like it there. Is that where you're taking me? I'll have to pack!"

"I happen to have found a little bit of Portugal, Agostino, here, in Essex, in Leigh-on-Sea. It's not Lisbon but it's near enough. Unless you have somewhere else in mind? I could always cancel."

"No way. I love Portuguese food and wine. Lead on."

Dónal drove to the restaurant. He wouldn't be drinking so driving her home afterwards was not going to be an issue. Nor did he want to presume anything by suggesting he leave the car at her place.

They got to the restaurant and sat in the small bar while going through the menu. Dónal asked her what drink she would like.

"Well" she said "I'll just have what you're having."

"I'm having a mineral water. I'm driving. Anyway, I'm cooling my boozing for a while."

"Then I'll have one as well. I'm not bothered one way or the other and knowing you as I do I reckon watching me sip cool lager wouldn't be much fun for you."

Then she did it again. She reached over and touched, no squeezed, it was definitely a squeeze, his arm. As if to say "it's ok, we're ok". The gesture disarmed and surprised and delighted him.

"That's settled then, two Buxton's it is, though I sometimes think there's more harm and poison in them bottled waters than in the whole of Guinness's brewery."

They were shown to their table and ordered some food. Both stuck to the seafood side of the menu – prawns in garlic and scallops to start and they both had the Dover sole. For a little thing, Angie was well able to put her food away. She ate everything with gusto and without embarrassment, something Dónal loved to see.

And they talked. They talked all the way through the meal, sometimes cutting into one another's account of some incident or other concerning the people, the characters they both knew from their shared world, the empire that is the UK Construction world.

They hardly tasted the food though both agreed the sole was the finest ever eaten. They shared each other's desserts and rounded the meal off with some strong, aromatic Brazilian coffee and a scattering of almond biscuits.

On the way back to the car Angie linked her arm into his. It was just so natural. It felt for both of them that there was no way ever again that they would walk together without they were so entwined and the thought crossed into their shared subconscious that they should have done this years ago and that all the time since was lost and wasted.

Dónal turned to her when they reached the car. He turned to her and he looked at her and she looked at him.

"Fuck this for an act" he said as he embraced her, pulling her into him, one arm about her waist and one hand on the nape of her neck. She looked up at him and her lips mouthed something just before he kissed her. He kissed her, one hand now lightly on her cheek. She gasped but she kissed him back. She kissed him back and all of her was given to him with that kiss just as all of him was given to her.

They parted and looked at each other for an instant.

"Bloody hell. What the hell was that?" Angie said.

"Fucked if I know but I want more of it. I've wanted it for years Angie but I didn't know it. I love you. I've been in love with you for I don't know how long. I know. I shouldn't have said that but it's true Ang. I love you. I'm in love with you. Really."

"And I may well be in love with you Dónal Doughnut. Yes, I do love you. I thought about it, about us, today, all day. I was afraid of it, afraid of you and afraid for me."

They remained in that embrace for a time. Just holding each other. Protecting each other. They might have remained there transfixed for all time but for a taxi driver who nearly reversed his cab into the pair of them.

Dónal drove them back to Angela's. They said little, if, indeed, anything on the way. She snuggled in as close as she could to him throughout the journey. Then, again saying precious little she led him by the hand from the car and into the house and up the stairs and into her bedroom and into her bed.

As soon as they were in the bedroom Dónal reached for her and held her and kissed her again. First, full on the lips, then exploring the inside of her lip with his tongue. She threw her back and giggled as he kissed her on either side of her neck. Her hands were on the back of his neck, massaging it while he ran his strong hands all over her upper body, holding her in close to him.

He held her breasts, feeling at last those those he had secretly ogled so many times in the office. He held her as he opened the zipper along the side of her dress, pulling the flimsy garment aside and revealing her green, silk, bra.

He moved the cup aside, revealing the pert breast, nipple erect, inside it. He touched her nipple, stroking it while looking down into her eyes.

"God" she mouthed "Dónal, Dónal" she moaned as he pressed more firmly on the nipple, kneading it on his fingertips until taking it fully in his mouth, squeezing the nut brown nipple between his tongue and lips. Her breathing grew heavier as shed moaned and sighed, her senses exploding as he opened the bra, leaving it fall from her shoulder. He slid the dress from her shoulder while she opened his shirt stroking his chest and pushing the shirt from him.

He held her away from him to see her. She was nude now from the waist up with only a tiny pair of green pants left on.

"Christ Ang, you're so beautiful. You're just so beautiful."

He made love to her for what seemed like an age. Slow, then fast then slow – stopping and starting and stopping and teasing, again and again and again.

"I never felt anything like that before. Never ever ever."

"That makes two of us then pet. That was something else Ang. Something else."

They lay on the bed then, spent, and not having the energy to draw even a sheet about her she turned into him and curled up into the crook of his arm. They fell silent for a time as their breathing became shallower and more relaxed.

"I love you Ang."

"I know" she sighed, "I know now."

With that they surrendered into a most wonderful, deep, contented sleep. Dónal was drifting into that tranquil place when he heard Angie whisper "and I love you Doughnut. I love you."

They awoke at daylight to the sound of the first trains to and from Liverpool Street. Angie reached over for him and placed her arm across his chest.

"Good morning Doughnut Man" she said, "what now?"

He drew her towards him and she slid over until she was lying on him body to body.

"Do you really have to ask? he said as she straddled him, mounting him and reaching down to place him into her. She rode him that way. Moving up and down on him. She was as light as a feather, it was almost as if she wasn't there at all.

When he tried to move in rhythm to her she stopped him. She placed a finger across his lips.

"Shush", she said "this one is for you."

She brought him to orgasm and afterward kissed him on the forehead before dismounting him and going to the bathroom. He could hear her humming to herself until the sound of the shower drowned her tune out.

Normally that would be Doral's cue to escape. Friday night's dreamboat was usually Saturday morning's nightmare but he was in no hurry to go anywhere that morning. He grabbed a quick shower once Angie had finished while she nipped to his car and brought in a small shoulder bag to him.

"You came prepared!" She said.

"It's my away strip" he replied "I never know whether or not I'll get back to my own bed the way I live and the way I work. I didn't presume anything. I hoped something might happen between us but I never thought we would be having breakfast together."

Angie raised an eyebrow "Are we having breakfast together then?"

"Come on" he replied, "there's a "Little Thief" on the Stratford roundabout. We'll get something there and see where the day takes us."

Neither of them had any plans so after breakfast Dónal drove over to Southend. They walked the full length of the pier doing a Terry and Arthur as they went.

"Good Gawd, it's the VAT Man Terry" Dónal said in a passable Arthur Daly voice. Angie ate candy floss. He had ice cream. They walked hand in hand or arms linked all the way to the end and pack again, telling each other about each other all the time.

They passed some seafront pubs.

"If I was in Southend on a Saturday morning I'd be in there. Beer and strippers and bar snacks. That's all I know in this country."

"You're better than that Dónal. You just got stuck in a rut. You'll break out of it."

"You're right Ang, dead right, but things are going to change from here on in. I don't care if I never see the inside of a pub again. It's unnatural. There are things happening now in my life that I never imagined could happen only a week ago. I must make plans. Plans that will include you."

"Steady on Dónal. We're not getting married just yet" Angie said bringing him down to earth.

"No" he laughed at her "we're going to have some fun first. You fancy a night on the town? I've not been up West in an age and there's a play on I think you might like."

"A play? In the West End? Och, I dinnae ken I would like tha! Me being from Glasgie an' all and no used tae sich."

"Come on it'll be a laugh. We'll stay up there and make a night of it. We can stay in The Strand Palace, it's a good hotel and the room rate is good. You up for it?"

"Yeah, I'd love to , you serious but?"

"I am. I got to make a call first though."

With that Dónal called the Savoy Theatre and booked two seats for the evening production of the Neil Simon Play. "The Sunshine Boys" then he called the hotel and reserved a room for that night.

"Let's go back for our gladrags gorgeous – we're going up the West End."

With that she did that thing again. That arm squeeze thing. It was her giveaway sign he realized. It gave away her happiness and his part in it. He looked at her and smiled. She winked backed at him and they walked along the promenade for an hour or so, not saying much, just enjoying each other's nearness.

Chapter Seven

IN THE WEST END

The night went off like a dream. They laughed their way through the play. Angela couldn't get over the fact that Danny de Vito and Richard Griffiths were live on stage in front of her. The contrast in size between the two actors added hugely to the comedy and Dónal and Angie were in stitches all during the show.

Angie found it hard to reconcile the rough and ready, unsophisticated, Irishman with the cultivated and cultured gentleman escorting her through The Strand afterwards.

When he brought her into a little Italian restaurant in Covent Garden, she half expected him to speak to the waiters in Italian.

"Alas, no" he said "now if it was a French restaurant I would get by but Latin bears little resemblance to modern Italian. The same is true of Greek."

"You know Latin?"

"Si, per omnia secula seculorem. Casam bulum jumka jo haira hanna mallacca" the words tripped from his tongue, astonishing her, "and classical Greek as well."

"No way, no way. You just made that up!"

"Alpha Beta Gamma Delta" he said "are the first four letters of the Greek alphabet. Do you want to hear it all?"

"Go on then. See if you can."

And with that he rattled off the Greek Alphabet, finishing with Omega. "Like the watches" he said. He even scribbled the letters on the back of the specials menu. She recognized some of the symbols. He wasn't kidding.

Over the meal he told her tales of ancient Greece and of the internal strife between the cities and their never ending battles with Persia.

"Like in the movies. Troy and such" Angie said.

"Not quite but yes."

"Brad Pitt, mmm, in a gladiator suit! Will you wear one of them for me? You could ravage me and say all them Greek words. You could have a big sword and a helmet. I can see you in a little skirt now."

"I'm shocked. Shocked. To think I had you down as a quite shy lass."

"You were right. Ah am a quiet, shy lass. You just bring out the devil in me."

"You say that to all the blokes" Dónal said, laughing.

"No I don't. Last night was different Dónal. I've done stuff but never went all the way like that. I wasn't a virgin, don't get me wrong but I never really let go like I did last night. I used to just go through the motions. I even thought I might be frigid or something, I had so little interest."

"Wow! That's told me. I don't know what to say. I feel ten feet tall anyway for a start. I'll be walking with a swagger from here on."

"No change there then" she laughed.

"I don't swagger. Well, maybe a little bit but that's only to annoy fuckers but now I'll have my chest stuck out, strutting, proud like."

"Well you should be. You succeeded where many have failed. You pressed all my buttons, and you a half savage from the bogs of Ireland."

"It was the same for me. Really. I got a bit carried away last night. Seriously though. More than a bit carried away. That's why I didn't use anything, I was just lost in the moment" Dónal said, lowering his voice.

"Don't worry. As it happens I'm on the pill. But not for contraception."

"I see" Dónal said and he mouthed the words "A Woman's Complaint".

"Something like that."

"Say no more. Does that mean we can get carried away again tonight then?"

"Why do you think I let you bring me here? There's a big double bed waiting for us in The Strand. You fit for another night of pure pleasure or must I pick up one of these waiters?"

Dónal paid the bill and walked her, quick time, back to the hotel. They said little the whole way but she held his arm doing that squeezing thing to him as they moved along.

That night in the hotel was as magnificent as the night before as they explored one another slowly and with more confidence. Discovering each other afresh and finding out how to please each other the better. Unselfish, giving and receiving in equal measure until falling asleep, as one, their lust and their love sated.

He awoke before her in the morning. He watched her for a time as she slept. Then he stole her from sleep with the gentlest of kisses on the cheek. She moved and yawned and smiled and placed her arm across his chest.

"Mmm, how long have you been looking at me?"

"Long enough to know I love you more with every breath you take."

"You're some smoothie. Tell me more though, I love it."

"Later sexpot, right now we have to talk" he said, "well, I have to talk and you have to listen."

"You're married. Dónal, you're married. Or you've got someone else. You shit. You said you loved me. Only a minute ago."

"Shh. It's nothing like that. There isn't anybody else in my life and I do love you. I love you so much I never want to let you go or let this moment pass. But I have to go away. Soon. I should maybe have told you before but I didn't want to spoil things."

"Where, go where? When? Why?"

"Fallon is sending me out to Abu Dhabi once we're finished in Bishopsgate. There isn't any work for us in the UK and besides I must sort something out over there. Something very important. I'll be back once everything is complete. I only found out about it for certain on Friday. I didn't tell you because I was afraid you would just blow me out."

"Yeah, blow you out instead of blow you." She pouted.

"It wasn't like that. Nothing has changed. I want you. I love you and I want to be with you. It'll be another month before we ship out so we have time to make plans."

"What plans? You're going to fuck off and that's that. That's the plan."

"No that's not the plan. That's not what I want at all. I want you to come with me. Not much for you to do out there mind. All day long by the pool. Then shopping in the malls in the evening and fine dining by night. It'll be tough I know but I'm sure you'll muddle through the day until I get back from toiling in the desert."

"You for real? Abu Dhabi? And Dubai?"

"Yup!"

"Wow. Double wow."

"You have to keep quiet about this for now though. We'll have to complete that work in Bishopgate first but once we get the instruction during the week we'll move things along sharpish. I'll let you know when to hand in your notice but don't breath a word of it until then."

"Shit. Andy will be pissed off with me".

"No. No he won't. He won't want to hold you back. He warned me to look after you, you know."

"He never did."

"He did. Corbett must have told him of the job in Abu Dhabi – they're thick as thieves,

"Now young Dónal" Andy said to me "it's none of my business but if you don't get hold of and grab Angie now, you'll regret it and so will she. You two are made for each other so seize the day and bring her with you to the land of shimmering sands. And treat her right" he said, honest."

"This is all going too fast for me. Slow down. Let me think."

"What's to think about? Say "yes" and I'll book the flight. I'll get you on the same flight as we're on. Wait till the lads see you coming on board. The Badger will have a stroke!"

"I can't just drop everything. I've only just moved down here. And I mightn't like it out there. All those Arabs. And all that heat. I don't like too much heat. I even got sunburnt in Falmouth. And what about a job? – can women work out there?"

"But you can drop everything Ang, you can! In The Emirates you can live as you do here, it's not like Saudi. You can google it up – check out the hotels – there's no such thing as a second class hotel out there, just different grades of first. And if you get too hot you can live indoors – it's all air-conditioned – there's even a ski-slope with real snow. I've seen it. Arabs in white robes skiing and throwing snowballs at each other, It's unreal. And I love you and I'll look after you and if you're unhappy I'll bring you home, first class on Gulf Air! But that won't be necessary I promise."

"I don't know Dónal, it's a big step."

"Come with me Ang come with me. We're meant to be together– We'll go on a jeep safari and watch the sun go down over the desert before spending the night under the moon and stars in an oasis and we'll make love on the beach to the sounds of the Muezzin calling from his minaret while the Indian Ocean laps over our bodies as we writhe in sands still warm from the heat of that day's sun."

"Well, when you put it like that! You sure you're not working for the tourist board over there, Mr. Dónal of the silver tongue?"

"Hold your whist" Dónal said and he sang in a passable Scots lilt "will ye go, lassie go?"

She went quite for a minute or two.

She turned and looked away then returned her gaze to meet his.

"Yes Dónal. I love you and I will take a chance with you. I'll go. I will go to Abu Dhabi."

"You have no idea how happy you've made me Ang. You are my world now. My world and my happiness. You complete me, you make me whole."

She reached over and kissed him and squeezed him again.

"You're welcome" she laughed. "You can buy me breakfast in return. Here, in the room!"

Chapter Eight

BISHOPSGATE

The next weeks moved along at a breakneck pace on all fronts. Dónal and Angie saw each other every day at work and carried on the pretence of a normal working relationship, much to Andy's amusement, while repairing at night either to Angela's place or to Doral's. They spent the odd night apart but they might as well not have as they spent ages on the phone to each other, neither wanting to be the one to hang up.

The Badger and Phil returned to site on Tuesday, as did Billy and Jimmy. The lads got everything set up down below for the delivery of grout as planned. The Resident Engineer inspected the tunnel and insisted a vent pipe or riser was placed into the chamber as a means of ensuring the void inside would be entirely filled.

The three lads together checked the container to see that their chocolate bars were intact after the weekend. Dónal asked if their secret was intact and both men nodded.

"For now you shouldn't even tell the wives" Dónal said "I've not told a soul like we agreed but I'm not married like you boys."

"If you were married you wouldn't say anything so daft, would he Phil?"

"Aye, that's for sure" Phil said, "sure no man would tell the wife about something like that. Don't I even burn my payslips so she doesn't know how much I earn? Money has a queer effect on them. They're worse than the taxman if you ask me, way worse."

"You're some pair of fuckers" Dónal said laughing.

"Anyway my guess is you'll tell your bit of stuff up the steps there before either of us opens our mouth" said The Badger.

"Fuck me but you don't miss much. How well you twigged that!"

They hung around for a little while then and headed away in mid afternoon. The lads to North London and Dónal to Southend.

On Wednesday morning the ready-mixed grout was delivered to site. Dónal had arranged with the City of London Police that a traffic management plan was in place. The grout pour was to be continuous so the four mixers had to line up one after the other. No mean feat in those narrow congested City streets. Even London taxis had difficulty turning there yet Dónal managed to keep the compound entrance clear and directed each wagon in and out amidst the honking and shouting of delayed drivers. Dónal ignored the clamour and kept the grout moving. At one stage a van driver from Billingsgate hopped out of his vehicle and had a right go at Dónal but when he squared up to him the driver took one look at Doral's demeanour and beat a retreat.

By mid-afternoon liquid grout spluttered and sputtered out of the vent pipe, signalling that the void below was completely filled to refusal. Dónal called Andy and the Resident Engineer to witness the fact that the chamber below had been demonstrated to have been fully grouted up. This they did and Dónal sensed they were glad so to do. The discovery of the chamber had caused them no end of grief and they were just glad to see progress.

Dónal stood the crew down on Wednesday while the grout was left to go off. He wasn't idle however as he had records and diaries to complete. And of course he had a couple of his famous memos to deliver, each of which Angie had to sign for.

At one stage Andy stormed in while Dónal was handing over the notes, full of bluster. He looked at Dónal over the rims of his glasses.

"Look at this" he said "you know anything about this Mr Dónal?"

It was a letter from Credit Suisse on its headed paper.

"Fuckit" Dónal thought, "we're caught!" He felt sick. His whole body shook, a tremor running through him.

He looked at the letter. It stated that, as a result of vibration and tremors arising from BGW works, the bank's alarm system had been triggered on a number of occasions over the previous week and that a number of sensors had been irrevocably damaged and would need to be replaced. Credit Suisse, the letter went on to say, was seeking reimbursement of any costs arising and a guarantee every effort would be made to ensure against future damage.

Dónal couldn't help but burst out laughing.

"Ah now! Andy. For Pete's sake! How're we supposed to burst our way through without causing some vibration? Pass that letter onto the Resident Engineer and let him reply."

"You guys should tunnel into that bank and clean them out while you're at it" said Andy, "and don't worry about it," he continued "we'll sort this out. I'll tell them to expect more of the same for the next fortnight."

"Once we get through the cellar wall and start to move past the bank the vibration should be reduced anyway. Wouldn't this be the right time to break in there though? I might see if the lads fancy a detour into a bank vault. Must be millions in there, Andy, millions."

"Angela, we need to reply to our friends in Credit Suisse, that's if you can tear yourself away from your mooning over Mr. Dónal here."

"He'd be so lucky. Mooning indeed!"

"Dónal" Andy said "don't milk the situation below. You've got a good sum in now for extras so crack on with it. I still need to get back on my overall programme."

"I'm thinking along the same lines Andy. We need to get that rig out of the ground ourselves and on a ship to Abu Dhabi."

"Where the bikini clad Angela will no doubt help you offload it!"

"You're a funny man, a very funny man, Andy. Anyone ever tell you that"?

"Yeah, hilarious" Angie chimed in.

"Go on kids, grab a coffee but do up that letter first Ang."

Angie stayed in Southend that night and Dónal dropped her into work the next morning. Then he set about organizing the travel arrangements for the three lads and himself to go to Abu Dhabi. Once he had the details he would book Angie's passage as well.

The full crew was on site so they set to work straight away. It took The Badger and Phil most of the morning to break through the cellar wall. The concrete was extremely strong, without any seams or cracks to help them work it. It was coming out as dust but the men stuck with it until they were fully into a face of grout. The grout was easier to work though and once in it they were able to take it out with pick and shovel. By the end of the shift they had advanced a total of four rings or nearly three metres.

The following day they built six rings in the grout. Andy was well pleased with this. If nothing else it showed the Resident Engineer that no effort was being spared and BGW couldn't be held to be "milking" the situation.

Progress the following day was similar but, as Dónal, observed, a slower rate of advance was inevitable once they hit the far side of the grout and hit concrete again.

This they encountered on that Friday evening. If anything it was an even denser concrete than before but the lads stuck with. The dust was everywhere and Dónal warned The Badger against lighting up down below.

"That dust is more explosive than coal gas lads. One spark and the whole lot could flash ignite and they'd be bring what's left of you out in a bucket."

Dónal placed an air mover in the tunnel and this eased things a bit but when The Badger and Phil emerged that evening they were covered from head to toe in concrete dust except for around the mouth and the nose where their masks had been.

Dónal gave a daily progress report to Andy along with completed, up to date, records.

"Never saw so much of you Dónal. Never in the history of BGW has any subcontractor's Agent been so keen to spend so much time in the office" Andy said "usually we can't pin you guys down. Any thoughts on this phenomenon Ang?"

Angela blushed at that. "Perhaps he's reformed." She said.

"He might have changed his behaviour a wee bit Angie, but reformed?"

"There's hope for me yet surely" Dónal laughed "there'll be great rejoicing in heaven when I repent, isn't that what it says in The Bible? Something about the repentant sinner."

"You won't figure in that scenario. You're going to the other place." Andy continued.

"I think I'd prefer it down below anyway. All that harp playing and Holy Joes up above. Not for me, that carry-on. Anyway, I knew a fellow who went to Heaven once and he couldn't wait to get out of it."

"Go on, why?" Angie asked as Andy groaned.

"He got lonesome so he came down out of it."

"Lonesome?"

"Yeah, lonesome. Sure there wasn't a sinner in the place. Ha Ha Ha! Get it?"

"Get out of here. Angie, don't let him past the threshold again today." Andy said, shaking his head. "Good one though. I'll work that one with the missus tonight."

"Best of luck with it Andy. You can tell her a dashing Kerryman told you that one. Meanwhile we'll continue slaving away while you get on with your more patrician lifestyle. We'll be through the chamber tomorrow hopefully. We're at the concrete again already."

"Good man Dónal, good man. I'll tell the RE. Don't be surprised if he pays you a visit. It's unlikely but be prepared."

By Saturday as Dónal had predicted they were fully clear of the chamber and back in a full face of stiff clay as before. Dónal logged the time they resumed normal tunnelling and prepared a sketch showing a profile of the tunnel as installed. They had less than twenty metres left to completion. Only five shifts if all went well.

Now he could concentrate his mind on getting the chocolate out to Abu Dhabi without any cock-up. He knew Kingdom Tunnelling. All he needed now was for some wanker in the yard to lay claim to his rig and before he knew it the container with the chocolate would be commandeered and whisked off to some other job.

Dónal left nothing to chance. He planned and organized the move, paying attention to every detail. His rig was shipped out in full and in three weeks it arrived in Mussafah, the Port of Abu Dhabi. At the dockside were Dónal, The Badger, Phil and Jimmy.

And awaiting Dónal in the Abu Dhabi Hilton was one Angela Morrissey.

Chapter Nine
ABU DHABI

Kingdom Tunnelling (Middle East) had an office on the tenth floor of a building owned by its sponsoring company, Darwish & Sons. The rented office was one of convenience only but without a local sponsor, foreign companies simply can't operate in a commercial sense in The Emirates.

Dónal and the gang had arrived in Abu Dhabi over a week before the Rig. This gave Dónal time to get the basics sorted out. Through Darwish & Sons, he arranged the issue of Residency Visas for all four of them. He knew Fallon would lose the rag over that as he had more control over the lads if they had visitor's visas only. Fallon had had revoked visitor visas before as a means of settling disputes but Dónal didn't want that particular Sword of Damocles hanging over his head.

Once he had a Resident's Visa he would be able to arrange one for Angie.

Again using Darwish, he arranged two large apartments in the Embassy quarter. They spent the first few nights in The Meridien until the apartments were ready. The heat got to Jimmy a bit at first but once he stared to acclimatize a little and calm down somewhat Dónal knew he would be all right.

He took the single roomed apartment for himself while the lads had a huge four bedroom one between them.

He contacted Kingdom's local man, Ravi, an Indian National from Kerala. Ravi was retained by Kingdom as a sort of general factotum. He spoke passable English and had a good grasp of Arabic as well as Farsi and Punjabi.

Ravi was charged with rounding up half a dozen Sikhs who would form the core of the crew once the work got underway.

Dónal hired two Toyota Landcruisers and a crew cab pick-up truck for himself, Phil and Ravi.

He called Angela twice or three times every day to hello and to keep in touch and just to hear voice. He texted her a "goodnight xxx" each bedtime before turning his phone off and was greeted by her "good morning xxx" when he turned it on each day.

Preferring to take it easy and relax the gang didn't go out at night until the third evening when Dónal suggested the head into the Al Ain Palace Hotel and have a few pints in the Ally Pally Bar and in the Irish bar, Finnegan's, nearby.

Dónal hadn't been in the Ally Pally for some seven years but as he walked in he swore the very same people were sitting in the very same seats as they had been all those years ago. They looked older and maybe the worse for wear but it was the same gang all right.

"These people must have great livers" Dónal thought as one of the barflies, an Engineer from Dublin spotted him.

"Look what the wind has blown in folks. It's the man from the Kingdom himself back to torment us. Mimi, get that man a drink." It was Tom Whelan, head honcho of the Ally Pally Gang.

"Mr. Dónal, it is nice to see you again. Long time now. You still drink Smirnoff Blue Large with small tonic, ice no lemon?" Mimi said as she hugged him.

"I wish Mimi, I wish but not now. No more vodka for me. I've seen the light. Just Bud please. Same for you lads?"

The others nodded and they joined the diehards.

"How goes it folks? I was just doing a roll call in my head as I came in. All present except for Robbie Power. I suppose he sent in a sick note?"

"Ah no Dónal. You won't have heard. Mr. Power is alas no longer on this good earth. He took ill over a year ago and he was buried within three months. Cancer."

"I'm sorry to hear that Tom. Still, I'm not surprised, if I'm honest."

"Aye, it's the way of things. We gave him a great send off. They sent his body home to Cork for burial."

"I never heard. I've been in the UK for the past few years. You know the two lads here don't you Tom? We've a new recruit here as well, Jimmy."

They shook hands all around and chatted about everything in general but nothing in particular when Dónal left them to it on seeing a large heavy set olive skinned man come in.

"Sharma, my old friend, salaam?" still keeping the Faith I see as Mimi set some nuts on the table Sharma was to sit at. She placed a bottle of Canadian Club and a glass with some ice alongside the nuts.

"Salaam Allah Khoum" Sharma replied. "Nice to see you again Mr. Dónal" Sharma said as he twisted the cork from the bottle and discarded it.

"Another glass Mimi" he said.

Dónal neither needed nor wanted the whiskey but to refuse would be to insult so he waited while Sharma poured two generous measures.

They clinked their glasses and sipped their drinks. It was the prelude to a negotiation and Dónal knew nothing would be agreed until the bottle was empty so they went around the houses a bit.

Dónal steered the conversation around to the price of gold and how it was traded. Sharma blinked at him.

"Only in the Gold Souk" he said. He would help. "Did Dónal want to buy or sell? The price in The UAE is controlled. What had he in mind? Some jewellery perhaps? For a woman? A man?"

"No" not jewellery. "Say an ingot?"

"You can buy such in the Souk also. They would be stamped and so forth."

"And if you were selling?"

"The same would apply. The stamps and so forth would be checked."

"Interesting" said Dónal "but say, just say, you had some larger, numbered ingots. Say it was old Nazi gold or such from the war. How would you get rid of that? How would you sell it?"

Sharma looked at him, his eyebrows raised, "Here," he said "I would go to the Lebanese. They are the best. Like the Jews they are always fighting with, only worse. But you cannot trust the Lebanese."

"But you are Lebanese." Dónal said

"Ah yes but I am good Lebanese. You need to talk to Bill Haslam."

"Rolls Royce Bill? I thought he was legitimate."

"He is. He is. But he is Lebanese first, legitimate second."

"I'll be seeing Bill before too long as it happens. I'll get his outfit to drive and place some piles for us and maybe subcontract the pumping to him also. Now I know where to sell my identity bracelet if I'm stuck. Anyway, to business. I'll be needing two at first then four mobile one hundred tonne' cranes. Usual rates."

"Prices have gone up. Labour is gone up. New rate is usual rate plus 10%."

"I couldn't be bothered arguing with you. 7.5% final offer? Drivers included."

"Agreed. Is fair."

"On site first thing Tuesday coming?"

"First thing – ok. No worries. Is fair."

"I mean it. No 'crane is late Inshallah' excuses. You guys use Allah when it suits you. Not this time." Dónal said, reminding Sharma of the delays caused on a previous job.

One of the difficulties of working in the Middle East was factoring in the amount of downtime due to prayer, especially during Ramadan. And delays were never the fault of the supplier but were always the "Will of Allah – Inshallah" and you daren't question same. "I don't want to hear "Bukhara Inshallah" on this job Sharma. The operators must be non Muslims. I can't have them stopping work to pray or refusing to work Fridays or Holy Days."

"I will see what I can do but Pakistani men all driving now. I cannot give preference to non Muslim. I cannot."

Both men took another drink but Dónal only sipped his while Sharma took more generous measures, emptying the bottle before making ready to go.

They stood up and shook hands. Sharma was a little unsteady. But not drunk.

"You are lucky I am good Lebanese Dónal" he said. "A bad Lebanese would notice you never wear a gold identity bracelet.

Never. Bill Haslam will notice Dónal. Be careful. I hire cranes, you dig tunnels. You get into buying and selling to Haslam, you don't know what will happen. He knows some people. Very dangerous people. From Palestine. You hear me?"

"Trust an Armenian before you trust Haslam eh?" said Dónal.

"And don't trust an Armenian at all" Sharma said, restating a standard Middle East dictum. "I will call you tomorrow or the next day Dónal"

"Inshallah" said Dónal with a grin.

Aaaah! Yes of course. Inshallah." Sharma laughed.

Sharma left and the others joined Dónal at the table. Jimmy wanted to go to the Irish pub so they walked the short distance across the pool area. Dónal hated Irish pubs with a vengeance but put up with the kitsch to indulge Jimmy this once.

"This, I hope, is the one and only time we end up here. Listen to that bollox up on the stage, an idiot with a banjo singing songs about the old country and some tragedy or other. A load of misery upon misery. If he misses it so much why doesn't he fuck off back there?"

"Steady on Dónal", Phil said, and then, to The Badger, "we better get him back to the hotel. The Canadian Club has taken over if you ask me. And he was doing so well, staying off the hard stuff and all. We better get him to bed before he starts mouthing off about things."

"What are you on about?" Dónal said, his speech slurred now. "What are ye all having to drink? Pints of stout all around, is it?"

The head barman, Anto, a Dubliner, looked at Dónal.

"Welcome back to Finnegan's, Dónal" he said "you must be just off the plane. You look tired out. Maybe you're a little jetlagged. I don't think you should have a drink just now. Why don't you let the lads take you home? Come back tomorrow. The girls will be delighted to see you then. Go on home now. Lads?"

With that the crew manoeuvred Dónal out the door and into a taxi. They walked him through the lobby of The Meridien and shut him up when he tried singing about gangs of men digging for gold in the street.

The lads accompanied him to his room, opened the door and threw him onto the bed. He swore a little. He cursed them and their mothers and all belonging to them before crashing out like a light. He started to snore and the others left him to it.

Chapter Ten

ARRANGEMENTS MADE

Dónal awoke the following morning at daylight to the sound of a minaret. He felt like absolute shit. At first he didn't know where he was but as he entered the conscious world and took in his surroundings he realized where he was.

"Abu fucking Dhabi! What happened? Sharma! That's what happened. Oh Christ!"

He went to the mini-bar and grabbed a vodka miniature and a can of coke. For medicinal purposes only!

"Oh shit. What happened last night?"

He drank the vodka. It tasted good. He waited for it to take effect. While he was waiting he mixed another and pieced together the events of the day and the night before.

He panicked at first at the thought he might have overplayed his hand with Sharma but as his recollection recovered he figured he had gotten away without too much collateral damage. Sharma would know there was something going on but he wouldn't want to know. He had made that clear.

Dónal was coming around. The liveners were having the desired effect. One more and he would be able to face into a shower.

He turned on his phone. Shortly thereafter it beeped the "message received" signal. "Good morning handsome xxxx" it read. "Four kisses" he thought and he smiled. She must have sent it at her bedtime. He would call her later. "She wouldn't want to be kissing me today" he said to himself. His breath stank and the taste in his mouth was foul. He hadn't felt like this for over a month. And to think he used to be like this every morning.

"Sharma was a one off. It was necessary. My hangover will pass. I will get better. I just need to detox. I'll be OK tomorrow. Today I'll feel like shit but tomorrow I'll be fine. Right as rain. Ready for anything. Ready for Bill Haslam. I've had a cure. No more booze until after the sun has set tonight. The holidays are over now boy."

He showered and headed for the poolside. At that hour of the morning there wasn't anybody there. He had the pool all to himself so he swam a few lengths. He struggled. The booze from the night before and from that morning was still in the system but the swim refreshed him somewhat. He chose a lounger in the shade of the nearby Forte Grande Hotel, closed his eyes and dozed for a while. He awoke about an hour later. It was just after nine. The sun was up now and he could feel its heat even in the shade. He swam again. Two lengths without effort. He was coming around and was starting to feel peckish – a good sign.

Jimmy joined him about that time. The culture difference hadn't fazed him at all. He jumped into the pool, swam, showered and joined Dónal.

"This place is better than Lanzarotte," he said. "Did you get breakfast? I'm starving."

"Good thinking Jimmy, you go and knock up the others and we'll grab some breakfast. We can get something here by the pool. You'll not get any black puddings though. Nor rashers of salty bacon nor proper pork sausages."

Phil and The Badger returned with Jimmy.

"You don't look as bad today as you did last night" Phil said, "you were in some state. I was sure that French girl you groped in Finnegan's was going to call the cops on you. Lucky we got you out of there."

"Aye" The Badger chimed in "if it wasn't for me stepping in her boyfriend would have lamped you. Big fellow he was and all."

"Now lads, I told you before never to kid a kidder. If I had some bit of stuff by the arse, she would have been beside me in the bed this morning." Dónal replied, calling their bluff though for all he knew they may have been telling the truth.

"You were in some state though. Anything could have happened" Phil said, laughing "you wouldn't to spend too many nights with that Sharma in the Ally Pally."

"I won't be making a habit of it" Dónal said "I've been in the water and I'll be taking it easy from here on in. I had to go through the motions with Sharma. He reckons Bill Haslam might be the man to help us in regard to our goods. I'm going to try and see him this evening or early tomorrow. We'll chill out today. One thing I've learned about doing business out here is patience. That and drinking cup after cup of that sweet shit they call coffee.

First, Dónal made a pre-emptive call to Fallon. He told him of the deal he had brokered with Sharma and that he expected to have some more news after he had spoken to Rolls Royce Bill.

"Where are you now?" Fallon said.

"In Mussafah. Just sussing out the job Ned" he lied "I hope Gordon put in some money for dewatering the shafts!" Dónal continued, going straight into the attack." We'll be pumping here non-stop!"

"It's in the desert, what water?" it was Gordon. Fallon must have been on speaker. "I hadn't allowed any sum for dewatering. You sure you've not just hit a wet spot?"

"The ground here is full of water. Seawater! And it's tidal. Like on the beach. Dig a hole on the driest sand in Blackpool and you'll hit water. Didn't they teach you that at that Quantity Surveying College?" Dónal said, knowing that would annoy Gordon no end, he could see his mouth opening and closing in his mind's eye. Huffing and puffing.

"No matter", Dónal continued I'll get pumps and dewatering gear from Haslam. I'll use the output to compact the sand about the shafts – that's called Hydrocompaction Gordon" he said, again to annoy "and that will save us bringing in loads of stone for the access roads."

Dónal started shaking the poolside table, making a racket.

"There's a jeep pulling in just now. Shit, it's the guys from the Oil Company, ADNOC, policing their Pipelines. We've no permits in place yet. I better go and chat to these guys. I'll talk to you later." He hung up at that.

"You're some boy Dónal. Some boy! No doubt about it." Phil commented.

"The less he knows the better for now. They'll not expect us to be out there for a week at least but I'm going to get Haslam's men out there as soon as possible. He has two Engineers, Tariq and Nidal. One of them can look after things out there once I've given them the line."

With that he called up Haslam Construction and asked for Mr. Bill, giving his name, in Middle East fashion as Mr. Engineer Dónal of Kingdom Tunneling.

"Ah Mr. Dónal. Salaam, Salaam. We heard you are come back to Abu Dhabi. How are you keeping? And Mr. Ned? And Mr. Jim?"

"We are all well Mr. Haslam, thank you. Thank you. And you. You are well?"

"Good. I also am well Inshallah. Please, please call me Bill. And I shall be pleased to call you Dónal."

This augured well. Allowing the use of familiarities at this early stage in their renewed acquaintance signified a willingness to treat, clearing the first hurdle.

Mr. Ned and Mr. Jim asked me to pass on their good wishes and their respects to you Bill. They asked that I might meet you and discuss a matter of business with you."

"Of course of course, but all in good time. Please, please be so good as to call in to our complex. You remember where we are, near the Maqta Bridge?"

"Yes, I remember. Near the bridge turn off. At the roundabout. You know we are doing some stuff in Mussafah for NMDC?"

Yes, I heard mention of it. Come here tomorrow morning at around eleven and we can discuss things. Perhaps, Inshallah, we may do some business then."

"That suits me fine Bill. Until tomorrow Inshallah."

"Sorted boys!" he said to the crew "we can relax for another day. Tomorrow we'll get set up in Mussafah."

Things were now moving along nicely on the job front. It was vital that everything on the tunnelling side of things went to plan. The Abu Dhabi end was critical to his plan and he explained this to The Badger and Phil.

"We must ensure nothing happens to cause suspicion. We'll move ahead with the job and make everything ready for the planned arrival of the gear. I'm thinking of really moving things forward on that score. If we pushed it we could double up on cranes and get the shafts ready early. It'll mean hiring in an extra piling rig but it'll look good. We need to be left alone to do what we need to do once the container full of chocolates arrives. The best way to do that is to get stuck in. There's nothing else to do here anyway.

I'll see Bill Haslam tomorrow as scheduled. We'll need to keep him on side but I'm not going to discuss anything with him other than the Mussafah job. The more I think about it the less I like involving him. We might not have any choice in the end but for now we might just be better off picking his brain. He knows his way about but this thing might be too big for him.

I'll ring Hassam Ali tonight. I reckon you'll have to go to his yard and pick out at least 1000 metres of scrap 1000mm Pipe. It's way more than we need but there'll be offcuts. Pick out the best of his stock. Get him to cut it before he loads it. I'll hire in welding and burning gear and the Indians will sort that out."

"Have you got hold of Ravi since? Has he organized Binda and his gang?" Phil asked.

"Sorted. The lads will jack up their jobs and come to us as soon as we need them. They're being very badly treated where they are. Usual story. You know Binda told me last time I was here that we were the only guys who didn't cheat them. He couldn't believe it when we gave them a thousand dirham of a bonus. It's sad really. They're first class men. I reckon we're lucky to have them."

"Come on, let's order up some breakfast. Smoked salmon and scrambled eggs all round yes? And some nice dry champagne to wash it down perhaps? Get used to it boys. We'll be living it up from now on!"

Jimmy looked puzzled. "You lads must be on a right good deal. Even with tax free dosh I won't be living it up. Can I have just scrambled eggs? I don't think I like smoked salmon. I'd like a few sausages all right though."

"Gold medal ones Jimmy?" Dónal said. The others burst out laughing.

"What the fuck is it with you lot and Gold Medal sausages? You were at the same crack over in London. I prefer Cumberland anyway. They're meatier."

"How do you like them? Fried in Kerry Gold butter until Golden Brown?"

At this the three roared out laughing, causing the staff and the other pool users to look over at them. Jimmy looked lost. He was embarrassed. He was left out of the joke and he knew it.

"Don't worry Jimmy", Dónal said, spotting Jimmy's discomfort "we're not having a go at you. It's just a story we heard. Your talk of sausages reminded us, that's all."

"I don't know what the fuck gets into you lot. Halloran was right. "The Three Stooges" he called you. Grown men laughing at nothing only your own ignorance. He reckoned ye were on the waccy baccy."

"Dónal is right Jimmy" The Badger said then, "we weren't having a go at you. It was just something stupid. Something of nothing."

"Ah go on away with ye! Maybe I'll try some of that smoked salmon so. I don't want any of that champagne though. I'd prefer a cup of tea with mine. Mind you, they can't make tea properly out here. I don't know what they do. It's the same in Lanzarrote. The tea is piss there as well. Go on sure, as I see it, I'll try some champagne too."

"You're right there Jimmy, good man," Dónal said keeping his face straight, "you can't get Lyons Gold Blend out here!"

"Come on" said Phil before he started laughing again "we'll get a bite to eat."

They spent the morning by the poolside, Dónal sticking with bottled water. In the afternoon they went for a spin in one of the jeeps out to the desert, to the dunes. The older lads had seen it all before but Jimmy was open mouthed at the scale of the mountainous hills. Dónal left him take control of the vehicle for a while and he let rip. Jimmy was just a big kid really and whatever residual anger he was carrying since the morning was soon forgotten.

The crew laughed a lot that day. Jimmy didn't realize it but his passengers were but prisoners on day release. Each of them laughed out loud and enjoyed the trip but none of them could quite eliminate from his mind the sense of anticipation and, if the truth be told, of foreboding, about the container that was at that very day ploughing its way through the Suez Canal, bound for Mussafah.

Chapter Eleven

BILL HASLAM

Dónal drove the length of Hamdan Street to Bill Haslam's offices outside the city in Maqta. Even though he had been there only four years ago, much of that wide boulevard was unrecognizable. He looked for familiar buildings and landmarks. Many of them had been refurbished and renamed, while more had been demolished and either had been or were in the process of being redeveloped.

It was non-stop. Recessions come and go throughout the world but Abu Dhabi steamrolls on. When its sister city, Dubai, embarked on its ambitious building programme on the back of anticipated tourist revenue and ran into difficulties it was Abu Dhabi, with its huge revenues from oil and gas that supported it, effectively bailing it out.

The huge Dubai projects, The Palms, The World and the Bur Jur Arab Tower, went ahead, albeit at a slower rate, nearly crippling the Emirate financially but it was Abu Dhabi that underwrote the lot.

Some years earlier, an Indian bank, registered in Dubai, the Bank of Credit and Commercial India, BCCI, went bust. There was a scandal but rather than have its reputation tainted, the UAE stepped in and resolved the crisis by recapitalizing the bank to the tune of billions. Dónal recalled how the state delayed all payment from its national companies for six months until revenue was generated to cover the shortfall. The consequence was that everyone was starved of cash meanwhile.

Companies and individuals were giving and receiving post dated cheques. It was a very crazy, very scary, time but Abu Dhabi supported its sister states and bought out the problem within the six months.

The cheques were treated meantime as a type of bond as to utter a cheque in the Emirates without having the funds to cover it was a criminal offence.

There was more to it than that of course. The Global economy, Saddam's invasion of Kuwait, The Taliban, Iraq, Iran, Israel, Palestine, The USA, Oil, Gas. The whole region was a nightmare of past, present and potential conflict. Fluid and ever changing, much like the wind sculpted desert where Jimmy had had such innocent fun.

Trade was the lifeblood here. Since the dawn of civilization the peoples of the Gulf had been buying and selling and trading goods, including slaves. Now the commodities were Oil and Gas.

But the one constant throughout the ages was and is that most precious of metals, Gold, and they would shortly be sitting on over ninety kilos of the stuff.

Bill Haslam's office was in the Darwish Building. Unusual for Abu Dhabi, the building was not a high rise monstrosity. The Maqta area was at that time an industrial quarter full of warehouses and contractor's offices. The more commercial high rise sector was on the city side of the bridge but Dónal guessed it wouldn't be too long before the advancing city would soon push the industrial area out beyond the port area.

The building was low sized, spacious and airy, well, air conditioned that is, but the architect had managed, by using clever windowscapes, to create a sense of openness, unlike some of the more claustrophobic structures all over The Middle East.

Bill Haslam greeted Dónal warmly, coming down the wide staircase to welcome him and shake his hand.

"Dónal, Salaam my friend, welcome, welcome. It is good to see you. You are well?"

"Very well, Bill, very well thank you. And you?"

Haslam waved his hand and they walked up the steps to Bill's offices. Once there Bill invited Dónal to sit in one of two massive armchairs facing Bill's equally massive desk. As a sign of friendship Bill sat alongside in the second armchair rather than sit opposite him across the desk.

"Tea, or coffee, Dónal?"

"Coffee will be nice, thank you Bill."

Haslam again motioned and a liveried office boy glided into the room. Bill said something to him in Arabic and the boy glided out again, this time backwards.

The two men made some small talk until the boy returned with a tray laden with a traditional round bottomed brass coffee pot and some glass cups along with a selection of Arab and Lebanese biscuits. There was a bowl of sugar cubes and, in deference to Dónal, a jug of either cream or milk.

Haslam poured the coffee and gestured to Dónal to have his pick of the sweetmeats and to try the coffee.

"Mr. Jim and Mr. Ned are both well?"

"Both fine thank you Bill. They asked me to pass on their greetings. Mr. Jim himself placed a wooden crate into our container for you. The finest of Irish Whiskey I believe."

"Then we will share some when it arrives. Paddy I hope?"

"Yes indeed. That's what Ned said. 'Bill will have no other'."

Dónal took one of the vilest sweetest marzipan sweets and placed it in his mouth. He rolled the foul tasting stuff around his mouth, and made to savour it.

"Wonderful, wonderful. As ever Bill", he said, "Imported fresh from Beirut?"

"From the plane this very morning. Baked at midnight in my home village by my own mother in a clay oven."

"Every morsel a masterpiece, every bite a revelation. These biscuits should be sent to the Queen of England and to the crowned heads of Europe, so they should." Dónal said though in his own mind added "to poison the fuckers."

"You are too kind Dónal, too kind. Please have more." Haslam said as he toyed with one himself.

"Bastard can't stand them either!" Dónal thought "What a bollox!"

"The coffee is of course Arabian" Haslam said as he poured some into the cups. He put no less than four cubes of sweet white sugar into his.

"Sugar?" He said, holding the tongs over the bowl.

"Just one please Bill" Dónal said, wondering how advanced Haslam's diabetes was. Never thin, he had certainly put on some weight since they last went through this little ceremony.

Dónal sipped the hot strong coffee as etiquette demanded and both men remained silent for the polite period of reflection etiquette also demanded.

"You have of course a list of your requirements Dónal?" Bill said at last opening the meeting.

"I have indeed Bill. Usual stuff. I imagine Tariq will assist us in this respect."

"I have already instructed Tariq to give you his fullest cooperation."

"You know the work is for NMDC. All payments from NMDC to us will be surcharged and your invoiced sums paid directly by NMDC to Kingdom Tunnelling on your behalf. This is a nuisance I know. I suggest you increase your rates accordingly by a full twenty percent. That way we both profit Inshallah.

Haslam laughed. "You know the system too well Dónal, much too well. The only fly in the cream will be the NMDC consulting Engineer, that Hans Van Boone. He will be very exact, very precise. You must ensure the line and level is good. No twists and turns like last time."

"Fair comment that Bill. I've got our lads to make sure the Pipes are of better quality. I'm ahead of you there. And it's "fly in the ointment", not "fly in the cream"!"

The two men exchanged some more pleasantries and some gossip, mostly about other contractors and about some of the more colourful characters among them when Haslam mentioned Sharma, almost as an afterthought.

"Sharma tells me you met in the Ally Pally? You should keep out of there Dónal. It has been the downfall of many a contractor, that Ally Pally. Sharma tells me you were enquiring about the price of gold. He tells me you might have some to sell?"

"Sharma was drunk. I don't know how we got talking about it. I think I was wondering how a robber would dispose of a bar of gold in Abu Dhabi. Before I knew it he was getting excited and telling me to ask you. It was nothing. I know I don't have any gold. I don't even know how we got around to the subject."

"I thought as much. It is very difficult nowadays to trade gold below the belt. You would have to have connections and be prepared to take a huge discount, maybe fifty per cent."

"It's "under the counter "not "below the belt" Bill". Dónal laughed again.

But Haslam was not for turning. "If you have stuff to trade then I can help Dónal. There is no market here in the whole of The Middle East for contraband gold. The penalties are severe. You cannot trust your own brother. The price is too high. Abu Dhabi Central Prison is not a very pleasant place."

"Even in Egypt now everything must be assayed. Same in South Africa. Gold, my friend. is worth a fortune indeed but you can't sell it unless it is legal. India is the only place where you might be able to get a decent price but only in small amounts there as the government is watchful. Pakistan is the same now. Ever since that Osama Bin Laden everything is out of the bounds. No more sweeping things under the mattresses."

"No worries Bill. Seriously. It was just an enquiry. Nothing more, nothing less".

They concluded their business at that and Dónal drove back to the hotel. "Haslam sure got very excited at the prospect of brokering a deal" Dónal thought. "but he might have left something slip when he mentioned India."

"Indiaaah!" said Dónal to himself aloud then. "India just might prove to be the answer."

He stopped the jeep and called Angie.

"Hello you" she said.

"And hello to you too. I'm only calling to say hi. I miss you Ang. I so miss you"

"Och. Away wi'ye. The sun's gone to your heed out there."

"That's as may be but you're the only real sunshine in my life, in my heart."

"I thought I told you to stop being such a smoothie! But go on, tell me more, I love it!"

"If things go to plan here you'll hear it every day and every night for evermore."

"Oooh, I'm dying, only dying to hear it. When are you sending my tickets? What was all that about the beach and the ocean?"

"Everything's good here. When can you fly out? We're still in the hotel but I'm sick of it there. We move into our apartments first thing in the coming week. That's Saturday out here don't forget. I'm serious. Get out here as soon as. It feels right Ang and I don't want to lose you. Not now I'm just after finding you."

"I've given my notice in so Andy knows I'm going. The girls in Billericay know I'm off but they don't mind as there's another nurse wanting to move in. I'll organize a flight for the end of the coming week."

"Do you want me to that from this end? You'll need to e-mail a copy of your passport to me and I'll get the local Thomas Cook to book the flight. From Heathrow OK? Leave the details to me. I'll get you a holiday visa and that'll get you into the country. Once you're here I'll make sure you get a residency permit."

"You sure about this Dónal? The flight costs a pile of money. Do you want me to pay? I want to pay my own way, really?"

"You sure you're from Glasgie?" Dónal laughed "Don't worry about the money side of things. All that is sorted. Just get that sweet smelling, firm, fit, gorgeous, sexy body over here."

"And there was me thinking you might like me for myself and my personality."

"Didn't notice any such, babe. I look forward to meeting them though."

"Bastard", she laughed and then, softly, "you will mind me Dónal, won't you?"

"Yes pet. Yes I promise. I will mind you. I will look after and protect you no matter what. No one or no one thing will ever hurt you or let you down ever again, not ever."

"Ok Dónal Ok. I love you and I miss you and I want to be with you. All the time."

"And I love you. God I wish I was there now. Just to give you a hug – here's one over the phone rrrrrrr!"

"I got it, I got it. Over all those miles I got it. I feel all tingly."

"Likewise pet, likewise. I'm going to hang up now or we'll be here all night and there are some Filipinas in miniskirts waiting for me!"

"And there's a big hairy Scotsman in a kilt waiting for me! See you Mr. Dónal!"

Chapter Twelve
A Meeting Arranged

On Saturday, the weekend over, Dónal and crew left The Meridien and moved into their apartment building. It was little bit removed from the city, in one of the better suburbs. Dónal had deliberately picked this vicinity as the American Embassy was within easy walking distance of the apartment. Not that asylum or protection within the grounds of the embassy was on the agenda.

Even though Dónal had sworn to ease up on his drinking, like every committed boozer he was keeping his options open and maintaining his supply lines. Ramadan was not far away and, during Ramadan, the city's bars shut down and the hotels and restaurants were not permitted to serve alcohol. Dónal knew of one or two restaurants where wine was served discreetly but a man would want to be fond of badly prepared and poorly served Mexican food to eat in such.

Now, from Doral's perspective, the good thing about the American Embassy was that it had, within its walls, a fine, well stocked, lively bar. The bar, Chesty's, after the famous American war hero, was for the use of the Marines stationed in the Embassy. They had an open night once or twice a week, partly as a public relations exercise and partly to allow the marines a chance to fraternize with some of the female ex-pats, nurses mostly, based in Abu Dhabi. Doubtless also, it helped in the Embassy's intelligence gathering role as there was no shortage of loose talk among and gossip amongst the barflies.

"I'm good to you guys" Dónal said as he brought the lads into Chesty's. "Once they get to know you it'll make it easier to get in during Ramadan. Don't make any smart remarks about Uncle Sam or you'll be turned away next time. On Thursday nights here the queue will stretch around the corner to the main entrance. The joint will be jumping and believe me when I say it's the only show in town."

There were only service personnel in the bar that evening. Their crew cuts gave the men away. The women, also in fatigues were identifiable by their shorter stature, though one or two of them could easily have fallen into either category.

Still, Americans on their home soil are nothing if not friendly and hospitable and Dónal and the gang had a most pleasant evening while making themselves known to their hosts.

Next day they drove to a large supermarket nearby. "You'll be delighted with this place Jimmy. You can buy some stuff here that is very dear to your heart," Dónal said as they parked outside.

He led them into the store. Groceries, local and international were shelved within.

"Fallon would come in here, buy four trays of Pepsi and fourteen thick rib eye steaks every week. He ate two every day, one for breakfast, one at night". Dónal said.

The others laughed at that, believing it of him, knowing the man as they did.

There were two sections marked "Non Muslims Only".

"Wait until you see what's in here Jimmy." Dónal said.

The first section was fully of displays of western foodstuffs. Ham, pork and bacon products mostly but lots of other items, even "Smoky Bacon" crisps, were on display.

The second area was a huge alcohol store. All sorts of beers and spirits were on display here.

"You must have one of these to shop here" Dónal said, producing his Liquor License. "Aren't you lucky you have your uncle Dónal to mind you now?"

They stocked up with enough food and beer for a small army and brought the lot back to the apartments. Though tempted, Dónal didn't buy any vodka, and, when they unloaded the goods at the apartments, Dónal made sure none of the beer was placed in his apartment, even for storage.

"I told you I was going on the dry boys. Well. So now for you! Put that in your pipes and smoke it! While you lot are going out every night I'll be stuck here watching reruns of The Beverly Hillbillies."

That evening, Dónal rang Angie. Everything was in place. She had received confirmation of her flight by e-mail and had checked in already. She was excited, he could tell from her voice and, try as he might he couldn't disguise his own delight.

They chatted for an age. Andy had organized a farewell party for her. The Contractor's staff and The Resident Engineer's staff had declared a truce and they had arranged a leaving gift for her and a meal and some drinks in a Cheapside pub. Nothing special but they really all made her feel she would be missed. She had cried a little, she told Dónal. She had no idea they thought so well of her. They even gave her a bouquet.

Dónal was delighted for her, "no more than you deserve, Ang, no more than you deserve."

"Andy said he would personally fly out to Abu Dhabi and do you harm if you didn't treat me royally. Then he said to say 'hello' to you."

They said their goodnights, intimate, soft, at one with another across the continents.

Before he turned in, Dónal made another call. It was to a private Dubai number.

"Hello" he said when the phone was picked up, "may I please speak to Mr. Saki Singh Chungh? It is a friend of his brother, Gian, speaking, I am calling to pass on Gian's good wishes".

"One moment please. May I please have your name and the nature of your enquiry?"

Dónal identified himself and gave his business as personal. Immediately on so doing he was put through to the man himself.

"Velcome, Mr, Dónal, Velcome. Gian said you vere coming to Dubai, coming to Dubai."

"Another two times tables" Dónal groaned inwardly.

"Yes, Mr. Saki. I met Gian recently in Southampton. He asked that I pass his greetings on to you."

"That is good of you, good of you. You are in Abu Dhabi now. Abu Dhabi? Gian told me to expect you, to expect you and to assist you."

"Yes, I am arrived in Abu Dhabi. There is a matter I wish to discuss with you. A private matter but one which might be to our mutual benefit."

"A private matter, a private matter. I see, I see." Saki said letting Dónal knew he understood Dónal wanted to meet him face to face. "Vill you come to Dubai? Or if you wish ve could meet in Abu Dhabi, Abu Dhabi. I will be there as it happens over the coming veekend. Perhaps ve could meet at my hotel, my hotel, The Hilton. Ve could have a meal and a few drinks yes, a meal and some drinks, yes?"

"That would be excellent Mr. Saki. I will meet you there at about seven pm on Thursday."

"Wery good, wery good, Mr Dónal. That will be satisfactory, most satisfactory."

Dónal turned his phone off at that and considered where things now stood. He reduced everything to basics:

On the job front all was going to programme.

On the Angie front all was going to programme.

On the chocolates front, enquiries were ongoing and a final decision pending. He had explored options on how to dispose of the goods and would go through these with Phil and The Badger but the more he thought about it the more convinced he was that it was his chance meeting with Gian that might provide the solution to the problem.

Chapter Thirteen
ANGIE IN ABU DHABI

Angela arrived in Abu Dhabi the night following. Dónal met here at the airport and boy, was he happy to see her. He hugged her again and again, embracing her joyously, squeezing her tightly to him.

"Here steady on, steady on" she said but her body language and her eyes spoke "don't stop!"

Dónal ushered her through the airport into a waiting Limo he had hired for her pick-up. She was impressed and said so, giving him her now signature arm squeeze and holding his hand as the chauffer pushed her luggage trolley to the car.

"Welcome to Abu Dhabi Ang. Welcome. Am I glad to see you or what? I missed you. I am so in love with you I don't know if I'm coming or going anymore."

She kissed him full on the lips then. "Likewise Dónal, likewise" she replied "I was afraid I might never see you again. I cried you know, I cried."

"Well, you're here now. You need never ever gain cry. From here on in it's feelgood time."

"I'll hold you to that" she laughed, saying "so where are all these famous shops at? I thought we might get in a few hours at the malls before I leave you ravage me to death!"

"We could do that if you want. Will I get the driver to turn into the city? Only I thought we might get the ravishing out of the way first. But if you want to buy clothes and such instead of having the gear you are wearing ripped from your body by these hot, strong and eager hands then so be it."

"Och, go on then. We'll have the ravishing the noo so. I promise not to think of Gucci or Armani or Dolce and Gabbanna while you have your wicked way wi'me."

"Your wish is my command. I thought we might treat ourselves tonight and tomorrow night so I booked us into the Khalidia Palace complex. It's quite a nice little spot. I knew it when it was just a small hotel on the edge of town but they've refurbished it since. I hear it's quite nice now" he said, "except for the cockroaches. I've heard they've never really gotten to grip with the problem. I've got some Biff-Baff powder to sprinkle about the room. It smells a bit but it does help. That, and the light. If you leave the light on in the room they'll not trouble you. They prefer the dark and keep out of direct light. You'll be able to hear them in the Air Conditioning ducts, munching and scraping and scurrying about. Just pay them no mind."

"And don't pay any attention to the odd gecko. That's a type of lizard. They get in through any window left open. Mostly they just cling to the ceiling. Last time I was here there was a pair of them in my apartment – I was drinking a fair bit. I thought I was in the horrors and had started to hallucinate but no, they were the Real McCoy.

"And the mosquitoes. You must be mindful of those little bastards, day and night. They'll eat you alive out here."

"Dónal, shut the fuck up! No wee beastie is going to intimidate me. Just tell that driver to put his foot down. I need ravishing and some retail therapy afterwards and then some more ravishing and then some sun and then some more ravishing. Aren't you glad I came?"

"Glad isn't the word for it babe, I'm ecstatic, over the moon. Over the moon. If you look closely at it you'll see me jump it."

With that he rolled the roof top open and above them was indeed a crescent moon, alone in the dark, purple, sky, save for a single star in its seeming embrace. She said little but squeezed and held his arm in hers.

He brought her to the hotel then, to a luxury suite in that most luxurious of hotels. They made love. They made love for an age. They made love with a true, deep, affection and with a longing and a hunger that overwhelmed them both, deliciously.

"Are you ravished enough yet?" he said to her, spent.

"For the noo, aye, for the noo."

They showered and bathed together in the huge Jacuzzi. They said little at this time, choosing to savour the sheer joy of just being together.

Certain of each other they lay in each other's embrace on the massive bed, he looking into her eyes and she into his, unflinching in that gaze. Neither saw any doubt for there was none. Nor was there any fear. And that trouble in her eyes had been taken away, banished for all time even though he had believed it to be permanent.

And also banished, from Doral's eyes, was that sadness, that emptiness of the soul that others had tried to relieve in the mistaken belief their attentions would alleviate it only to find their love, such as it was, proved no solution.

Though tired, they did not sleep. Though thirsty, they did not drink. Though hungry, they did not eat. They just lay there, together, in silence, allowing their thoughts free roam. She to fancies of her future life with "that reprobate Dónal" and he to fancies of his future life with his "Glasgie Lass".

Eventually, Angie stirred him.

"You were starting to snore. You never snored at home. You tricked me into coming here. You're a secret snorter."

"I don't snore. I never snore."

"Well you snore now. And you better stop or ah'm awa' hame!"

"You're having me on. You just want more nooky."

"Well, now that you mention it. But can I have a real ravishing this time please. A right good rooting. All that lovey dovey stuff has put me in the form for a good shagging. Then you can bring me for some food."

"As I said, your wish is my command, my little bundle of joy" he said.

They showered, separately this time in case they got carried away again though neither had in truth much energy left.

They dressed in uncomplicated, comfortable, clothes. There were some twenty restaurants in the hotel complex so Dónal asked Angie to pick a number between one and twenty. She drew the Japanese restaurant overlooking a tropical garden complete with wooden bridges and a pagoda.

They had some noodles and sake to start, the strong warm rice wine hitting the spot and ordered some enormously expensive Kobe Beef. Dónal had eaten Kobe Beef before and he watched Angie's reaction as she took her first mouthful of the unbelievably tender, incredibly tastful and fantastically flavoursome meat.

"Oh my god!" she said "I never say OMG but that is just so good. Better than sex – well, not better than sex with you but OMG this is so good. I'll never again crow about Scottish beef being the best."

"It is something else isn't it? They massage the cattle every day to tenderize the meat. I always think of that scene in 'The Hitchhiker's Guide to the Galaxy' when they bring the cow to the table!"

"I never got that movie. It's a blokes' thing isn't it?"

"Yeah, I suppose, funny though."

They talked incessantly throughout the meal. She full of chatter, asking questions by the new time, about Abu Dhabi mostly and their future. She was looking forward to the whole Abu Dhabi thing but couldn't help but wonder whither afterwards would they go.

Dónal made to reassure her. He understood her concern. Even though they were certain of each other she had a real, practical, need to know where they were bound. She had made a huge sacrifice for him. She had take a major risk and, on the spur of the moment and because he loved her so, he felt he had no option but to balance her risk by being wholly truthful and honest with her.

The gold was always on his mind at some level or other. He nearly wished they had not found the cursed stuff. He had to tell her. If only to reassure her he had to tell her. There could be no secrets between them from here on. He had to tell her. It was as simple as that.

So he told her. Over the mango flavoured sweet cream he told her the whole story from beginning to end. Or, at least to where the story then was, leaving nothing out.

He told her, as she stared, wide eyed, incredulous, at him, of how they had found, hidden and moved the treasure. Treasure which was, even as they dined, on the way to Mussafah wherefrom, all things going to plan, they would ship it to india where they should be able to sell it for the bones of three million Euros, split three ways.

"I knew you were some bullshitter Dónal, but even you can't expect me to swallow that one."

"It's all true babe, all true. I'm sworn to secrecy so don't let on you know owt. Remember when we hit the obstruction and I sent all those "please be advised" notes? Well, that was when we found it. That's why we pushed ahead with the tunnel instead of milking it and holding up the whole show like Andy expected. The whole thing is driving me mad. I had to tell you. I felt like I was lying to you, not telling you. Well, now the cat's out of the bag!"

"More like the genie's out of the bottle, seeing where we are. You're for real, aren't you? What have I gotten myself into here? I thought I was coming for a holiday. Now it looks like I'll end up in an Arab jail. A far cry from "midnight in the oasis", more like Bairlinnie by The Gulf!"

Dónal laughed at her" "Nothing like that will happen pet. I'm a realist. At best, we'll have more than enough to start out and live with some ease from here on. At worst, we'll end up with a tidy profit. I often thought I'd like set up my own business. This might be that chance."

"Ok then" she said, nonplussed, "I'll have another dessert, Mr. Euro Millions!"

Chapter Fourteen
ABU DHABI PORT

"" The holidays are over now boys. Rise and shine and greet the dawn of a new day." Dónal said cheerfully on entering the apartment "our ship has come in. We're Mussafah bound."

With that the crew stirred themselves and, in the fashion of men everywhere, yawned stretched and farted before coming to order. The Mosques started up just then as the first glimmer of sunlight lit the lightening sky. Being on the eastern fringe of the city the mosques in their suburb were the first to begin the daily call to prayer. Then, one by one, moving from East to West, mosques throughout the city joined in, lending to the daily cacophony of the muezzins as they encouraged the Faithful to devotion and prayer and supplication to the will of Allah.

"How do they put up with that caterwauling every morning?" The Badger said. I have a headache from them in the morning and just when I'm feeling right they start up again. Five times a day they go off. Wouldn't you thing once a day would do them?"

"I don't think it was them fellows gave you them headaches" Jimmy piped up "I reckon you've a sore head after all that rum you drank last night".

"Well, hark at that, boys. Hark at that" said The Badger. "Wee Jimmy no less! Making smart remarks! Him that wouldn't say boo to a goose back yonder. That nurse in the American Embassy has made a right little maneen of you. A right little maneen! She must have squeezed your syringe right and proper."

Jimmy reddened and the others laughed.

"Better than pulling my pudding like you lot!" Jimmy countered.

"OOOH" the others went.

"This happy breed, this happy breed." Dónal thought as he led them towards the jeep.

He drove out of Abu Dhabi towards the new Port of Mussafah.

"Hard to think boys, this whole place" Dónal said "was a desert the last time I was here" the others interrupted him as one, completing the sentence, in hoots of laughter.

"Wankers" Dónal said "comedians and wankers!"

Dónal called Tariq. Tariq confirmed the cranes and excavators were on site. His men were at that minute offloading some pipes and measuring up same for use in the tunnel.

Dónal called Ravi. Ravi confirmed he had collected Binda and his crew and all were present and on site in Mussafah.

On arrival at the Port Control area, he produced both personal identification, in the form of his Passport and Residency Visa and Company Identification in the form of a letter signed by Ali & Sons. He presented the Bills of Lading, the Consignment Notes, the Customs Clearance Certificates, the ADNOC Work Permits and confirmation of their contract with the Abu Dhabi National Marine Dredging Company.

All the documents presented had to be examined and stamped in the Port Control Office. Dónal sat and waited in the thankfully air conditioned front office while the clerical staff, exclusively Indian, exclusively male, went through the completed forms paying meticulous attention to each and every page and to each and every entry therein.

Armed police and customs officials came and went through the office as Dónal sat and waited, outwardly patient and calm while inwardly fretting and anxious, to be called.

Other importers who came after he arrived were released while his papers were still being processed but he tried not to make anything out of this as their requests were most likely routine and related to everyday traffic.

Still, as the minutes ticked by, loudly it seemed, on the large office clock suspended from the low ceiling, he could not stop himself wondering whether the container had been opened. A spot check here would be unlikely but what if the stevedores had dropped the container during offloading, spilling the contents all over the dockside? Without thinking he fingered the key he held to the container as if it was a rabbit's foot, wishing for the consignment an unimpeded, swift, easy passage through the port.

After what seemed an age, though in reality was but an hour, he was called forward to the counter where, with a great flourish of rapid and energetic stamping by the station clerk he was handed back his documents.

"All is in order. Your goods are cleared for entry to the United Arab Emirates."

"Thank you Sir. You are most efficient. May we now collect the container?"

"You goods are most certainly cleared for entry but you may not bring them in until the final Entry Permit is signed by His Excellency Sheikh Bin Rashid Al Zayed."

"When please might that be sir? Or how might arrange this Permit be signed?"

The clerk accepted Doral's deferential attitude, as Dónal knew he would.

"His Excellency is coming in one half hour today at the very most. It is better to wait now. If you go and return there may be an unaccountable delay."

"Half hour" could mean five minutes or five hours in this part of the world. Dónal and the crew waited one hour. Then another. Then another. After a full three hours had passed and Dónal feared the offices would close for the midday rest period, a large Mercedes Benz SUV drove right up to the entrance to the complex and a young man in traditional Emirati Dishdasha and Headgear emerged. He signalled to Dónal.

"Salaam Mr Dónal. It is a time since we last met."

"Salaam Allah Khoum Mr. Faisal, how are you? It is indeed too long since we last met, much too long."

Faisal, a member of the upper echelon of Abu Dhabi's ruling elite, had, as part of his training as an Engineer, spent over a month with Dónal off and on when Dónal was last in Abu Dhabi. He had found Dónal to be very helpful and very practical. Dónal had not simply humoured him as many others did.

Faisal was now a nominee on many of the Emirate's National Enterprises. He was one of the more progressive young Princes, destined for advancement and, by virtue of his family to hold a suitably high position in the Nation's Government.

The Indian clerk looked shocked. He would have paled or blanched if such was possible. To think he may have delayed a friend of the Prince!

"Mr Dónal" Faisal said "you must come to my house. I am married now. Only one wife yet. I have two sons. It will be wonderful to have you one evening to dinner, wonderful."

"Of course I will come. It is indeed an honour. It is most unexpected and the more appreciated for it."

"Then it is settled. You will come to my Abu Dhabi house in one week from today. Are you alone or will there be another? One of your many nurse friends perhaps?"

"No Faisal, not a nurse! But I do have a special friend just arrived. Might she be invited also?"

"Of course, of course. That will be perfect. Just perfect."

They exchanged business cards. "What a stroke of luck!" thought Dónal as Faisal uttered some instruction to the office wallah who submitted the permit for Feisal's signature.

"This man has been courteous to you Mr. Dónal? You were not in any way inconvenienced?"

Dónal looked at the clerk. The clerk was shamefaced and fearful. One word from Dónal and he would be shipped back to India, his prospects ruined. But Dónal was not a vengeful man. If anything he saw the funny side of it and so he told Faisal that the clerk could not have more helpful and that he was in fact lucky to have such a loyal and dutiful servant. "Plus" Dónal thought, "that guy won't hold me up again. Not for any reason now. No way!"

Faisal signed the clearance certificate with a flourish. He made his goodbyes as he entered the offices while Dónal collected now signed documentation from the miserable, now humbled, clerk, who was now entirely deferential towards Dónal.

"We have already been delayed here" Dónal said to the man, "please ensure our goods are not held up at the exit gate."

"I will personally most definitely make certain no further delay will arise in this matter" he replied as he picked up the telephone and barked some instruction into it.

"Thank you for your assistance and your efficiency and courtesy. I will make sure to mention again to Prince Faisal how helpful you have been."

"If you wait just one jiffy I will have one of men accompany you to the stevedoring area. You might not find it a simple matter to locate your consignment. My man will identify your container and arrange most immediate loading for the onward transportation."

Dónal, The Badger, Phil and Jimmy repaired immediately then to the terminal proper and, with the help of the attendant, found the Kingdom Tunneling container among the thousands of others stacked there. It was stacked beneath two others.

The attendant asked Dónal whether he had arranged transport from the Port and, when Dónal advised him one of his contractors would collect the container, he insisted such was not necessary as His Excellency the Prince had himself ordered that every assistance be rendered him.

Within minutes of their arrival the huge overhead gantry crane had swung into motion. The containers above the Kingdom Tunnelling one were moved aside and restacked. Their load was swiftly picked up and moved along the length of the aisle where it was dropped onto the back of a waiting truck. The attendant asked Dónal where he wanted the load delivered and, on being given the site address, directed the driver to proceed to that location immediately and without delay. "Jeldi. Jeldi. Hurry. Hurry." He shouted at the driver.

Dónal motioned to the driver to follow him and they drove straight out of the Port area without any further stop or check. Dónal breathed a sigh of relief.

"That was some stroke of luck lads" he said "I was shitting a brick in case the container was opened. The Abu Dhabi Central Prison ain't too far away from here – last time I was here one of our lads got locked up for a driving offence. I had to visit him. Not a very nice place. No indeed. Not a nice place at all at all."

"Sure there's nothing in the container only the tunnel rig" said Jimmy. "Why would they lock us up for bringing that through customs?"

"Billy Halloran left his porn in there" Dónal said, thinking quickly. "That's a no no here. I hope you didn't bring any of your wank fodder with you, come to think of it. We wouldn't want to have to be visiting you in there."

"I'm not the one who needs that stuff. I'm sorted out. Not like you guys."

"OOOH" the others went at that.

"You're worth your weight in gold on this job Jimmy. Worth your weight in solid gold!" Phil laughed.

"That's what that nurse said as well."

They carried on in this vein until they arrived at the turn off to the first shaft. Sharma's crane and driver were on site as were Haslam's men. They offloaded the container and Dónal and The Badger opened it for the first time since it was locked back in London. It seemed like it was an age since they had

"Make like everything is normal boys. We're here to do some tunnelling work so get stuck in." Dónal said. "But first" he continued "let's check that our chocolate has travelled OK."

Together, they moved and shifted the equipment in the container. Binda and his guys helped and within the hour they had the bulk of the stuff moved out.

"Leave that Bentonite where it is for now lads" Dónal said, "we won't be needing it for a time yet."

Telling him to bring some drinking water Dónal sent Jimmy off with the surveying target as he made a show of setting up the theodolite. He told him to stand the target about 100m away, near the ADNOC perimeter fence and to stay there until he signalled him.

Once Jimmy was at a distance and Binda and the gang were cutting pipe, Dónal, Phil and The Badger moved the Bentonite out of the way, Dónal passing the bags back one by one to the others.

"Fuck me", he said, "it's not here. It's gone!"

"What are you talking about, you bollox. It must be there." The Badger said pulling Dónal out of the way as he strained for a look."

"Ha Ha! I had ye going there boys!" for there, in the back of the container, in the selfsame sandbags Dónal had passed out through the hole in the cellar wall under Bishopsgate were those nine, beautiful, bars of solid gold."

"Would you look at that" Phil said. "Just look at it. We did it boys. We did it. We're home and dry. I had my doubts Dónal but you pulled it off. Fair play to you. Fair play!"

"Aye, fair play to you Dónal. I put it out of my mind all along but them bars there mean I can go fishing from here on in. And Phil can go farming. And you can go courting that young one and maybe buy her a ring. Aye, good man, well done!" The Badger added.

"We're not home and dry yet lads. I know I'm not normally the cautious type but since I stopped serious boozing I've become more realistic. We have to sell the chocolate and that might be another day's work."

"Quickly now before Jimmy melts out there. Move the bars into my jeep. We'll keep it in the safe in the apartment. I reckon we'll have to get it to India to sell it though. I was thinking we might use Ravi to find a buyer. At least he knows the lie of the land over there and I know he's not above a bit of smuggling. People mostly, but I always reckoned there's more to that guy than he lets on. I don't know if we can trust him mind. He's Keralese. A convert to Christianity but I reckon under the surface he's pure Tamil and those guys have a long long history, much of it extremely unpleasant."

"Listen Dónal" Phil replied, "we've got this far. Ravi's not the worst of them. I would prefer Binda and the lads but their English is very poor. And they're illegal here so flitting in and out of the country might not be so easy. It's a case of the devil you know, isn't it?"

"My thoughts exactly. We'll use him but watch him like a hawk. Once he's in the picture he won't be able to take a shit without one of us watching."

Chapter Fifteen

AN INDIAN PLAN

Dónal asked Ravi to come along to the office that evening on the pretext of sorting out some details related to his visa application. He made a show of filling out a form and assured him the matter was a formality only.

"Mr Shoukie of Darwish & Sons will arrange everything and soon you will be granted a residency visa like the others" Dónal told him.

Their business in Darwish concluded, Dónal brought Ravi to the Red Lion nearby where Phil and The Badger were waiting. Ravi was delighted with this. This was a real step up for him, to be treated as one of the crew, as one of the Europeans. They had a few beers together when Dónal broached the real reason for Ravi's presence.

"Suppose Ravi" Dónal said, "just suppose, I had some gold to sell. Where do you think would be the best place to sell it?"

"The souk, Mr. Dónal, the gold souk is the best place. Prices are the same in Abu Dhabi and Dubai. Maybe a little better in Bahrain but not much better. No, not much. You have some jewellery to sell? Or to buy for Miss Angie perhaps?" Ravi said, the eyes rolling in his head as he shook it vigorously.

"Say I didn't want the gold to go through the souk? Say I had ten kilos or more to sell but could not prove ownership? Say I wanted cash – dollars or euros or sterling. What then?

Ravi laughed. "Now you are a Silly Billy Mr Dónal, only big businessman or a sheikh would be able to pay cash for such an amount. But they would need to see papers like a bill of sale. Even then a swap for diamonds would be preferred. But cash, in UAE, no way. Not now. Not since BCCI Bank time. Not for that amount. Unless it was sold in small bars – maybe 100g bars assayed, one at a time to different dealers over a long time but big bars no way, big bars, big amounts no way. Unless you brought the gold to Thailand or Hong Kong but even there it would be checked. The best place is India. No questions asked there if price is right, no questions asked, absolutely certain and without a doubt."

"Say I decided to sell the gold in India! How would I go about it Ravi? I mean I would have to get it there first off. Then find a buyer I could trust. One with enough cash to pay for it. Then I would have to get the money out of India. In dollars or sterling?"

"It could be most definitely arranged. By Jove. Most definitely. From Abu Dhabi Indian ships and dhows cross the ocean to Cochi all the bloody time without any checking whatsoever. No pirates this far north. Even if Indian Coast Guard stops boat, captain will fuck off again for $100. For £100 he will even escort you into port. Thiravandenum is best place to sneak into. Cochi is watched but Thiravandenum, no controls. I know this as this is how I come and go.

"You fucker Ravi. We pay you for your flights! Anyway, go on!"

"Is perk of the job Mr. Dónal, perk of the job" Ravi said, the beer making him that bit freer "you have your perk, I must have mine. Anyway, what was it I am saying? Oh yes. No problem bringing gold into India and no problem absolutely by Jove no bloody problem selling it in Cochi or in Munar. Or Mumbai. Mumbai is best. Much trading in Mumbai from old days when all the tea in South India was traded there for gold and silver then. Many jewellers there. Many thieves also but many traders too. No question asked."

"In Mumbai, people go into the drains and shovel out the old mud every night from the gold souk. Many years ago the dust from the gold workers clothes is being washed into the gullies. Now the scrap dealers are buying this mud and taking the gold out of it. These peoples would know who would buy gold. Oh yes. Big market but price very high now. More difficult to sell gold when price is very high as buyer is afraid price will drop and he will make loss! You will have to sell below market price. Maybe 50% below."

Dónal looked at the others before proceeding to say, in Irish. "Fear glic, nach ea? Ná dúirt mé sin!?" he said of Ravi. Both

Phil and The Badger nodded. Ravi was indeed a clever man, a very clever man.

"Are there any such fellows nearer than Mumbai, Ravi? Mumbai is a long way to go. Too many people there. Would a trader come to Cochi?"

"That is possible of course. I will straightaway make a telephone call if you wish. I will arrange everything. I can get a boat to take us from Dubai. Only Dubai. Not Abu Dhabi. But from Dubai no problem. Trading boat to Thirevandenum is best from Dubai. I know a man I use. Binda knows same man. Very cheap. Cheap is better as no one pays attention. Small payment to Harbour Captain is all and no stopping by coastguard is required."

Phil had meanwhile ordered some more drinks. Ravi fell quite as the lounge attendant, a fellow Indian, went about his business. Once the man had gone out of earshot, Ravi continued "you must be very careful when you discuss matters such as this in public Mr Dónal. There are many bad people around and about" he said. He was becoming excited by the prospect of making a huge profit and was, by virtue of the fact he was in a bar with Europeans men and being treated as an equal, quite emboldened. He called the waiter back and ordered another round of beers and, to prove his superiority, ordered, in English, some more nuts for the table.

Dónal was secretly pleased by this. He hadn't quite trusted Ravi sober but seeing him drunk reassured him that Ravi was neither better nor worse than any other man. He would have to be watched, and watched closely, that's all.

Dónal left them to it at that. He had a woman to look after and some love tokens to cash in.

The following morning Dónal took Angie for a spin to Al Ain. Al Ain is an inland city. Set in a huge oasis, the place looks spectacular green against the desert backdrop. It is the hometown of the ruling Zayed family, hence its importance. The city is overlooked by the Hatta Mountains. The oasis is the source of the bottled water sold throughout the Emirates but other than that is of little commercial significance.

"Wait until you see this Ang" Dónal said, turning off the highway and heading towards the nearby hills. They drove on a steep incline upwards along a winding twisting three-lane asphalt road for about ten miles. There was absolutely no other traffic on this highway other than their Jeep. As they climbed they could see, at times when the road crested outwards, a building above. Eventually, they arrived at a huge car park on a plateau atop the mountain.

At one end of the car park, at the mountain edge was a huge wall with a large entrance gate in the middle of it.

"Wow", Angie said, "it's like the one in the Milk Tray ad."

"That it is" Dónal said. "Funny but that's just what I said when I saw it first. Behind that wall is a palace. It is built on the highest point in the Emirates, making those who dwell therein closer to Allah. Also, it overlooks Oman and, in the Arab, world this lessens the status of Oman in some weird way."

He drove closer to the edge.

"Now have a look at that" he said pointing at what at first glance looked like it might be some sort of communication mast protruding from the rear of the building. "That," said Dónal is quite possibly the most expensive gazebo in the universe."

For there, leading from the palace, supported by a pair of struts, was a covered walkway, Some fifty metres long, it was a propped, strutted, pergola leading to an octagonal, shaded deck.

The old sheikh built this at Allah only knows what expense as a statement of his wealth. The road, the carpark, the palace, the walkway were all constructed to show his people and his neighbours just how wealthy he had become.

"I have no idea how much this lot cost, there is something obscene about the whole thing. When you see the conditions the poor Pakistanis and Indians who built this place live in you would have to wonder. Yet the poorest Muslim working here would see the construction as part of God's plan. Their poverty is as Allah decrees therefore it's all right."

"Hmm" Angie thought aloud "you're right. It is really awful. Here are we living in first class accommodation while the poor outside have little or nothing. It makes me feel bad somehow. If I had the chance I reckon I'd do something to help them."

"Maybe we can." Dónal said. "In our own small way maybe we can."

"How do you mean?"

"Well. Once we offload the gold, we'll have a shitload of money. More than we'll ever need for ourselves. I'd like to set myself up in business. I'm not ready to retire yet. We'll be okay. Once I have you I have all I want. Maybe we could start a charity or something. Put the money to good use. You know what I mean? I don't know what I'm saying really. I'm just thinking out loud."

"You really are full of surprises aren't you Mr. Dónal. I thought I was coming over here for the high life with some first class loving thrown in and now I find you'll have me scrubbing the walls in some makeshift orphanage in Delhi! Well, as long as I get the first class loving bit I'll row along with the rest of it. I love you Dónal. I see the good in you. Good that you don't see in yourself."

With that, on that plateau in the highest point in the Emirates, they kissed and embraced. They might have taken it further but they were interrupted as three choppers flew overhead heading towards the palace. Dónal and Angie waved furiously at them.

"Do you think that was the Sheikh?" Angie asked.

"No. If was he would have seen you and landed and taken you in to his harem to made a sex slave of you. He would have had me put to the sword while imprisoning you to use and abuse at his whim."

"Sounds interesting. Do think the Sheikh will be flying over anytime soon? All this goody goody talk has made me horny!"

With that they returned to Abu Dhabi, to the apartment, where they made sweet love, both of the tender and the savage variety, in the late afternoon, between the afternoon and the dusk callings of the muezzin.

Afterwards, instead of heading for a restaurant, they walked to the nearby shopping area and bought some street food – Lebanese Chicken from a roadside rotisserie and pitta breads and peppers.

"Get used to it babe" he said "we'll be slumming it from here on."

"No way! Not just yet. We have to do a shitload of highlife stuff first. I mean, we have to have it good first so we'll understand the sacrifice we'll be making."

"You're sort of like a smoked salmon socialist. Or like Saint Augustine. He said "Lord make me chaste, but not just yet". I know your type."

"I don't like the sound of that 'being chaste'. No way. Now 'chased', by you, that's OK. I reckon I could live with that but 'chaste' doesn't do it for me. Not at all, at all!"

Dónal laughed. "You can take the lass out of Glasgie but you can't take Glasgie out of the lass" was all he could say. With that she squeezed his arm. And with that, he knew they were fine and he knew she was happy. And that really, was all that, in the moment, mattered.

Chapter Sixteen

DUBAI

Dubai Creek is one busy place. New quays and additional docks notwithstanding, the creekside wharves continue to attract huge amounts of commercial traffic, mostly from small crafts, old and new, plying the ancient trade routes of the Gulf and the Indian Ocean and the Arabian Sea.

Ravi led Dónal, Phil and The Badger along by the spice souk and the huge vegetable market to that part of the quayside where ocean going dhows were tied up, their owners and operators awaiting hire or charter. Ravi signalled to one such and a wiry, wind burned, barefoot, Indian, wearing a strange collection of clothes – a Keralese Sarong under a Planet Hollywood t-shirt beneath an Afghani cap, approached.

Ravi introduced him as Moussa, "a most capable and reliable seafaring gentleman of his long acquaintance and one who could most definitely be relied upon to transport without notice that item for consignment."

"And us", Dónal said, "you, me, Phil and Tony. We all travel together. Does he speak English?"

"No English. Very ignorant man from backwaters. No education in that place. Only boats. People there born on boat, live on boat, work on boat, die on boat. Some fish, some move goods for trading, some smugglers."

"Ok, ok. Arrange a price. Haggle with him like normal. Tell him to sail his junk to Mussafah and collect us there the day after tomorrow. Give him 200 dirham for now, balance on our safe arrival in Kerala."

"What about return? We will want boat to bring us back. It will take two days to drive to Munar and back again. You will not have visa for India. Moussa must wait in port all that time. No problem most definitely he will wait for all that time if we give him the instruction" Ravi said, offering to broker the deal.

"There's always with an angle with Ravi, always with an angle", Dónal thought.

"That's fine Ravi. Good thinking." Dónal said however, keeping his thoughts to himself. "You sort out the details. Just be sure his boat will cut the mustard."

"Cut the mustard? By Jove yes. The boat will cut the mustard ok. And cross the sea to Thierevandenum no problem. And cut the mustard also."

Their business complete, the four headed back to Abu Dhabi to the site in Mussafah where Dónal had left wee Jimmy in charge of the site. In fairness to him he had looked after things and the shaft work was progressing. Both Sharma's men and Haslam's men tended to slacken off if unsupervised but Jimmy's presence kept them busy. They had the shuttering all but completed and they would be ready for concrete late on the morrow.

Dónal made a show of checking things. Was the concrete ordered? Did they have enough pipe cut and fabricated for the first drive? Did they need more stone laid about to allow the concrete wagon turn about? Was the concrete skip working? Were the bowsers full? What about the line and level of the shutters?

Everything was as it should be.

"Millions of dollars worth of gold and a gorgeous bit of stuff awaited him in the apartment yet he was still out there, in the desert, organizing and managing the bits and pieces that pulled the job together. "Why do I bother?" he asked himself. The answer to his question, if the truth be told, was because he loved it. Complain as he might at the end of the day he got a buzz out of it. There was a quite satisfaction in setting up a piece of work and seeing it through. It is an everyday challenge and one he quite simply lived for and loved except when his drinking got in the way. With that he climbed into the jeep and made for road.

"Mind you don't strain yourself" he heard Jimmy shout after him as he drove off.

"Cheeky fucker" Dónal laughed as he gave him the finger. "I'm heading off for a bit of nooky just now, and maybe some ice cream afterwards. I'll save you a bit".

"You can keep the ice cream. I'll look after your bit of stuff for you if you want though. She'd prefer a young buck like me I reckon. An ould fella like you wouldn't be of much use to her."

"What would you know about it? That old boiler of a nurse has it all over the Irish Pub that you shot your load before you got your jeans off the other night. She reckons you were a virgin before she met you and she had to work hard to make sure you weren't one when she left. She said you could only go at it the once. She had to work hard to get you stiff again and you weren't much use even then. She had to tell you not to worry, that it was all right."

"How come she's meeting me tonight then smartass?"

"Must be for a bet! Or a medical experiment. Or pity! Don't be surprised if she brings a few other nurses along. See if they stare at you. They'll be feeling sorry for you if you ask me. You might even get a sympathy shag out of one of them. Could work in your favour you know! Some of them nurses are just dying for a ride! They're desperate, if you get my drift! They'll all reckon they could make a man out of you, you know, sort of break you in. You should seize the moment! Make hay while the sun shines."

"Ah fuck off. I done it loads of times. Loads of times! In London, and in Donegal too.

"I believe you Jimmy. Thousands wouldn't but I believe you. Ha Ha!"

Dónal headed back to Abu Dhabi then, to the apartment where Angie was chilling out by the poolside. He changed into swimming trunks and joined her.

"That's all my men busy and working hard. Slaving away under the desert sun for the greater good of Kingdom Tunnelling Middle East Plc." He said as he joined her.

"I thought you were never coming back. I'm bored now. There's only so much of this sunbathing lark a gal can take you know."

"Yeah, I know, I know. To think you could be back in London, stuck in a site office with the rain bucketing down. You have it tough, no doubt!"

"I just missed you. That's all."

"Likewise pet, likewise," he said, taking her hand and bringing her to the pool."

While they swam, he outlined his trip to Dubai for her and the arrangements he had made to get their bars of chocolate to India.

"Can't I come? I would so love to see India. It would be a real adventure. Being smuggled in on an Arab boat. I could dress up like a slave girl. Or a coolie with a Chinese hat. Or a turban. I have a British passport so I would be OK there. You have an Irish one, I bet that's of no use if you're stopped."

"No way. It's too risky. I'm not sure how it's going to pan out over there. We'll be in Ravi's hands until we get rid of the stuff. Then we have to get back. It's no place for a woman."

"Who do you think you are? John Wayne? I'll do better than you in the heat – look at you, you're melting even though we're in the water. Anyway, I don't want to be left here on my own worrying. I'm coming and there's an end to it. We're in this together aren't we?"

"No. No. I'm not putting you in harm's way. No way. I've got to do this my way. I'll only be over there a few days at the most and the phones work so there'll be no need to worry."

"That's bullshit Dónal and you know it and you know I know it too. If it's too risky then I'm not letting you go. If it's not too risky them I'm coming along. This isn't like the U2 song. There's no room for the "with or without you" line. It's "with me or not at all", so there, put that in your pipe and smoke it, Mr. Dónal."

"Shit. I don't know Ang. What if it all goes pear shaped?"

"We'll fix it if it needs fixing but you're not going over there on your own. The boat will arrive tomorrow and we'll cross the sea together. End of."

"That's me told then" Dónal said reaching for his phone. "I'm to meet a certain Mr. Saki tonight in The Hilton. You might as well come along. The others don't know anything about him or about my dealings with him. I've decided to call in a very old favour. If we get into lumbar over there, he may very well be the only one we can rely on."

"That leaves the afternoon for a bit of scrimmaging then" Angie said. "All this sunshine and heat is making me hot. Hotter than usual. And the talk of India has made me think of the Kama Sutra. Come with me to my Casbah now and I'll be your harem slave – you can do what you want with me for one hour. God I'm desperate for it, you Bastard. No one has ever had this affect on me. Come on, come on."

Afterwards, as the sun dropped quickly to the horizon, they sat together on the balcony outside, sipping some hot, sweet, lemon tea, as the muezzins began the call to prayer.

"I love this time" Angie said. "It's so peaceful. Especially after making love. It just feels so right, so perfect. Don't let anything happen to destroy it Dónal."

They sat in silence then until darkness enveloped them and it was time to meet Mr. Saki.

Chapter Seventeen

A SIKH ENCOUNTER

The Abu Dhabi Hilton on Corniche Road is close to the Khalidia Complex where Dónal and Angie had passed her first night in the city. The Hilton however was still the preferred hotel of the business community who viewed the Khalidia complex as a holiday park. And. while the Al Ain Palace attracted the boozing ex-pats and the chattering classes, the Hilton remains the more discreet venue where serious business deals are made. It is also the favourite address of the wealthier members of the Indian community who identify with the Hilton brand as a symbol of class and status.

Mr. Saki was there, in the lobby, before them. He was dressed in full, formal, Sikh evening wear. Resplendent from the elaborate gold and white turban to the immaculate slippers, he cut an impressive figure, tall and elegant. He had been seated in an armchair towards the centre of the lobby and rose with a flourish of his robes on seeing Dónal.

"Goodah Mr Dónal" he said before turning to Angie and bowing to her from the waist before taking her hand and lightly kissing the back of it.

"And Goodah to you also Miss Angie, if I might be so bold and welcome, welcome" Mr.Saki said, keeping her hand in his for just that second more than convention decreed. "And please call me Saki and I shall call you Angie. And you I shall call Dónal. For we are friends and we can dispense with all formalities. It is a great pity my vife is not here to make us four but alas she is in Amritsar attending a charitable function on behalf of distressed Punjabis."

Saki motioned them towards the bar.

"I thought we might have a drink first. Or we could go directly to the dining room?"

"No, a drink would be lovely" Angie replied for them both, taking over.

"First class, first class" Saki replied, "excellent."

He motioned them into the nearby lounge and, as soon as they were seated, insisted on ordering a sweet port wine as an aperitif for them all.

"I prefer beer myself I must confess" Saki intimated "but formality requires protocols must be observed."

"Well we are now on first name terms now" Angie said, "so we could if you wish dispense with all such formalities. I think our Dónal would also prefer a beer. Go on, have one. I'll just have a mineral water though. Beer would fill me up before we eat."

"Dónal, if you take my advice you will never let this girl out of your sight. She has read my mind in an instant. It took my vife many months to do that!

"All men's minds are easy to read" Angie rejoined "all men think about is women and food. Oh, and horses or cars or sport of one kind or another. It's never anything important. I bet your wife had you sussed straight away. She just gave you a bit of time, that's all."

"Don't mind her" Dónal said, "I often think about work. Well, maybe not often but once in a while at least."

"No. No. She is quite right, quite right indeed. I think my vife did indeed have me sussed out as you say from day one. But that is the beauty of it all. Now ve have six children. Four sons and two daughters. Perhaps if she hadn't sussed me out ve might not have succeeded."

With that Saki ordered some beers and a mineral water and they made their way to the dining room for a sumptuous buffet meal.

They didn't discuss business over dinner. Dónal reminisced a bit about Saki's brother Gian and Southampton and how Gian had prospered there, becoming quite a figure among the Indian community and a leading supporter of the Sikh Temple.

Saki stroked his fulsome grey beard as Dónal told tales of Gian and of Gain's eldest son, also called Saki, and the scrapes he was forever in.

"That boy is too handsome. That is the root of all his trouble. He should have been married off years ago but England is too free a place. Too many temptations. He doesn't even wear a turban and his hair is cut. I don't know what will come of it. His father is the same. Gian only wears a turban now at festival time. And he cuts his hair. You would not know they were Sikhs except for their bracelets." Saki said, showing them his own, plain metal, bracelet.

"It is difficult for them" Angie said, "growing up in England and going to school there. We had lots of Indian boys and girls in our school. Some of the parents were very strict and their kids were miserable while the ones who were more relaxed seemed happier."

"As children maybe. But later, as adults, they don't know who they are. It makes them angry. They have no identity. They are British on the one hand yet Punjabi on the other. A man cannot serve two masters."

And then, addressing Dónal he said "You are Irish Dónal. You understand this problem I think. The British have never understood it. Never!"

"Maybe so." Dónal replied. "All I know is that peoples and cultures will intermix. If they do so willingly then there isn't any problem. Only if people are pushed will there be trouble. It has always been this way and it will always be this way."

"You should have been a politician. With sayings like that you would be hailed as a Political Guru or a wise man, a savant, in India."

"Politics is for fools" Dónal said. All I know about is work and money. Politicians are liars and manipulators. Even the more idealist ones become corrupted by power and twisted by the game they must play. Even a man seeking to do good must often lie down with the dogs and if you lie down with the dogs you will end up with fleas."

"Well spoken" Saki laughed. "And you are right. But you will never change it. All the revolutions and all the prophets and all the charities yet the poor are still with us and will always be with us."

"It's the same in Glasgow" Angie said. "As soon as one slum is knocked down, it is replaced."

"And in India. Every night in Mumbai the municipality clears a shanty town yet be midday the next day it vill be rebuilt."

The meal over, they retired to the bar for a drink and to discuss business a little. Angie did not make her excuses and leave as Saki expected but stayed with them.

"Tomorrow, said Dónal, I have arranged for a dhow to transport us and our merchandise across the ocean to Kerala. Our man Ravi, says he will introduce a buyer to us. My concern is that we could be walking into a trap. I need someone to watch my back over there. Someone I can trust not to interfere but will be ready to step in and help if necessary."

"As I said to you Dónal, this business is not my business. I could arrange things for you in Punjab but there is unrest there. You and your trade would not be a secret for long. Kerala or Mumbai are your best bet without a doubt. You should get in fast and get out fast. No sightseeing or dillydallying for Angie on this trip. You will be five or six days at sea on an open dhow. It is no place for a woman. Angie cannot go. I will put two of my men along with yours. You have some Sikhs already I think?"

Dónal nodded. "Yes, Binda and Moussa are Punjabis."

"Then you will have four Sikhs. That, my friend, is an army, an army in itself."

"If all goes well, you will of course be well rewarded for your part. The return from the sale after costs must be divided three ways. For your protection I think 10% of gross is fair. We may also need help with currency. A suitcase or two full of Rupees is worth nothing outside of India!"

"10% is too little Dónal. For exchange and protection, normally I will need at least 40%. But because I like you and I like Angie, I will agree 25%. I will as you say watch your back until you sell the gold. I will continue to protect you until you return and I will exchange your Indian money for sterling pounds also. Gold is very expensive now. Nearly \$2,000 per troy ounce. 25% is a good price, protection included."

They shook hands at that. The deal was fair. Everyone gained and neither felt cheated.

Dónal made to leave with Angie but Saki wasn't having any of it.

"Regardless of how our business developed this evening, I took the liberty of booking a room for you both earlier. One of the finest honeymoon suites in The Abu Dhabi Hilton. Please accept this small indulgence. A gift between friends, yes?"

"What can I say to that?" Dónal replied. "But how did you know Angie would be here? How did you know she was even in The Emirates?"

"Ah my friend Dónal, you have much to learn about our ways and much to learn about doing business in the Middle East. We look after our friends. Our friends are our business. It is our business to look out for you, it is in our interest to protect you, to do this we must keep an eye on you, if only for your own good."

Dónal just shook his head. Angie just laughed.

"Go now my children. Go to your bed. I have some calls to make. It is now two hours since I spoke to my vife. Her spies are better than mine. If I don't report in she vill be on the phone asking me about the beautiful girl in the Hilton whose hand I kissed. She will even know I was wearing my good turban and bana. I am not the only one with spies! It is a hard life."

Chapter Eighteen

THE DHOW TRIP

Their chartered boat sailed into the Dhow Harbour adjacent Port Zayed. As it happened, Dónal had been involved in the construction of the sea defences to the harbour during his last tour of duty in The Emirates and he was familiar with the area. The gang was waiting at the dockside and assisted in tying off the dhow.

"Will that thing get us across the sea?" The Badger said, scratching his head and grimacing.

"It had better" said Dónal, "it looks a bit ropey though. A bit the worse for wear. The ropes and rigging look half rotten."

"It looks rough I grant you" said Phil, "but its trim is good. And those lads on board have the feel for that boat. Look at how they move about on it. Nice and easy. No panic. Born sailors."

"Well, they do make the trip every week or so, full to the gunwales of all sorts of cargo. I suppose it'll be all right" Dónal replied.

"And these lads look to know what they're about. They came in here under sail. Never used the engine at all until tying up" Phil observed. "That's a skill in itself."

"Well, for good or bad, this is what we have. Where's Ravi? He should be here by now."

As if on cue, Ravi arrived in the pick-up, sporting a ridiculous looking yachtsman's cap. It had a gold coloured plastic anchor on the front.

"Captain Ravi at your service Mr Dónal. Today we will all be sailing people."

"Ravi! What the fuck? Where did you get the cap?"

"I am buying this first class hat in the souk only this one day over. It is good. You approve?"

"It's the business Ravi, the business."

"While I am there I acquired some second hand ammunition boxes also. I am thinking they are exactly the right size for our merchandise. Two will fit into each box with strong handles and they will not be noticed by any nosey parkers as everyone is using these boxes for tools and all sorts of nuts and bolts."

"Good man Ravi. The stuff is in my jeep. We'll put it into the boxes now before loading them on board."

Ravi and Dónal completed this transfer quickly and quietly and Phil and Ravi moved the boxes on to the boat where The Badger stacked them around and about the mast. He arranged them to form a settle for himself, lit a cigarette and sat down to guard their precious cargo.

"Look at your man" Dónal laughed, "he's like John Wayne riding shotgun on a stagecoach."

"Someone has to look out for you fellows. I won't sleep a wink nor take my eyes off those boxes until we offload them across the water. How long will we be at sea Dónal?"

"No more than ten days at the outside. We'll be offloading the chocolate this time in a fortnight maximum. We'll have to tack about a bit to get into the Cochin area and avoid the coast guard if possible but Ravi will sort them out with some backsheesh if they stop us."

The Badger lowered his voice and made sure Ravi was out of earshot.

"He's not beyond turning us in to the navy for a reward that Ravi – keep an eye on him if we do get stopped."

"Like it or not we're stuck with him. But for now, our interest is his interest. It's in India he'll make his play. We'll be ready for him though. I have a trick up my sleeve to deal with him if he tries anything."

The trip would be long and boring and hopefully uneventful. The Dhow was surprisingly roomy on board, being one of the larger ones. The northwest monsoon filled the lateen sail, assisting the diesel engine and soon they were heading north, hugging the coast. By evening they had passed Dubai and approached the Strait of Hormuz as darkness fell. The coast line was lit up at intervals all the way along and there was a huge volume of traffic both onshore and offshore.

"How will we stick two weeks of this?" Dónal said.

"Be thankful you're in still waters. On a trawler we're often at sea for longer. You just have to learn to be patient. Watch your skin out here. You'll be red raw from the wind and salt alone without any sun. We're not really at sea yet. We're still in The Gulf. I bet you there'll be a fair swell out there in the Indian Ocean" Phil replied.

"Aye, the ocean looks nice and calm when you're sitting on a beach looking out at it" The Badger said, adding his tuppence worth, "but things happen at sea. If the wind gets up out there who knows what'll happen? Do they get typhoons out here? That Indian Ocean is alive with sharks. I hope I drown before I'm ate alive. Imagine those bastards eating you limb by limb. You would scream then Dónal, scream while the bastards gutted you for your liver."

"My liver wouldn't do them much good" Dónal said "and no, they don't get typhoons out here, nor hurricanes neither. Nor tornados for that matter. I'm rigging up a sun screen for myself and I'll be watching movies and sports on my iPad. There are a few beers in the hold – I got Ravi to make sure I had a stockpile. If you guys behave I'll let you have some. Follow my motto boys "foolish is he who stands in the sun while he can sit in the shade". It's party time so relax and enjoy the trip."

Not having much choice in the matter, the lads made the best of it. They sank a few beers and the conversation ebbed and flowed.

Once they were through the Strait they headed out to sea as the morning sun rose to face them. There was some noise in the water and the lads gaped at a shoal of flying fish leapt out of the water not thirty metres from the boat.

"Look at that. There must be fifty or more of them fellows. This is the first time in weeks we've not had to listen to those bastards calling us to prayer." Dónal said, capturing the moment on his iPhone.

He sent the image to Angie with an x and a message saying they were ok. She would still be asleep he reckoned so there was no point disturbing her at that hour. He was wrong though as his phone trilled.

"Hello babe" he said on her answer. "We're going OK and are out in the Indian Ocean just now." There were guffaws from behind as the lads eavesdropped.

"I got your photo. Wow. I wish I was there with you. Or you were here with me."

"I know I know. Same here. This is just a hello. I can't really talk with the gallery here."

"You can tell me you love me surely. I need to hear you say it."

"I do I do. You know I do."

"Then say it. Tell me lover boy and I'll do things to you on your return you only dreamed of in your wildest wet dream."

"I love you" he whispered.

"Louder, like when you come."

"I love you" he spoke, at which a huge cheer went up from the crew.

"Now, listen to what you've done. You've turned a crew of normal idiots into a crew of gibbering ones" he said, holding the phone aloft as the lads howled.

"I'll make it worth your while big boy Dónal"

"Go on. I'll talk to you later when I find a quite spot on this tub."

Dónal went back to his iPad but the others needed another hand to play a game of twenty five, so they set to it for their usual stake of a pound a corner.

"We should really be playing for a grand a man" Dónal said "given our new found wealth."

"We're as poor or as rich today as we were back yonder" said Phil "I won't be counting any chickens just yet so a pound a man it is as per normal. You're not in Monte Carlo yet Dónal."

"Maybe I should be, my luck is in" said Dónal, as he turned the trump card, revealing the Ace of Hearts. "My rob I think" said he laughing.

"Jammy bastard" said the Badger as he led off with a low diamond.

They played like that for an hour or so until the heat got to them. It was too hot even to argue the toss or complain about each other's mistakes at the table. All they were fit to do was lie in whatever bit of shade they could find and sleep.

Ravi had warned them of this, telling them they should try and rest during daylight hours and eat and sit about at night. He was right. The first couple of days and night were a torture but come the fourth night they had settled into some kind of a routine. The inescapable heat had a wearying, weakening affect on them all however and Dónal, not having sea legs, became quite sick . Really sick. Worse than he ever was after a feed of booze. Laid low sick. The crew had more or less ignored the passengers since setting out but one of them produced a potion of some sort on seeing Doral's distress. Whatever it was, it did the trick and by day seven he was much, much better.

They had made good time however, picking up the tail end of the inward monsoon as the sailed past the Lackshadweep Islands on the ninth day.

"Two more days from now Mr Dónal and we will be landing in Lighthouse Beach in Kovalam. That is very good place to land with a fine harbour. I have arranged already a taxi. I suggest you stay for two days in this place. There is a beach resort here where no question will be asked about visas or passports if I am coming with you. You will need to rest there before completing our mission."

"Any thoughts about the next stage Ravi. Mumbai or Munnar?"

"I believe we should avoid Mumbai. That place is full of thieves. Munnar is definitely better place. Cochi also good but many police and soldiers here also. Munnar is quite place with good trading. And is not far. Only one half day in minivan. I vill of course drive. Nice drive through the mountains. You vill see all the tea and rubber plantations and the teak forests. There vill be tea picking at this time of year. Kerala is a very beautiful place. "God's Country" it is called. Very fertile. Very rich. Not all like the rest of India."

"Sounds good to me Ravi. Looks like you have it all planned and prepared."

"Well, yes and no Mr Dónal. You will have to be calling the hotel with a credit card number as I could only book the rooms on the provisional acceptance. Ask for Mr Peter and tell him about our connection. He will look after things most very vell then by Jove."

So they lay up in Kovalam for the coming two days, taking rooms in the Mararikulum Beach resort where they got a much needed rest in comfortable surroundings. Mr. Peter did indeed look after them very well by Jove. They swam in the pools and longed about the place like normal holidaymakers except for one member of the group, The Badger, who always stayed in his room along with his boxes.

"I've minded them too long" he said "to have them nicked by some ragged arsed thief now that we nearly have the stuff home."

Dónal switched his phone on. He had turned it off at sea and had left it that way save for his calls to Angie. There was an amount of missed calls – from Sharma, Tariq, Bill Haslam, Fallon, Corbett amongst others. He called Tariq first.

"You were looking for me Tariq?" Dónal said. There was a problem with my phone.

"Everyone is looking for you Mr Dónal. Including that Prince. I was wanting to tell you the first shafts are completed now and we are ready to move to the second locations. In fact we have now already commenced the move with Sharma assisting. No one has seen you for one week. Sharma was worrying."

"Thanks Tariq. If your men and Sharma's crew continue the work we will be ready to begin as soon as the pipe is fabricated" Dónal bluffed. He didn't give a shit how the job was going. In fact he had more or less forgotten about it but he would have to return to the Emirates and he didn't need any complications there.

He called Sharma and listed to him bleating for a while until he cut him short by telling him he had left a cheque for him with Ali & Sons for collection in one week, at the end of the month as normal. Sharma wanted to meet him of course but that was only so he would have company in The Ally Pally. Dónal told him he was in Dubai but they would have a beer when he got back.

He called Fallon. As expected, Fallon barked a series of questions at him in regard to progress, complaining about Dónal being incommunicado over the past fortnight. Fallon could smell a rat. He probably reckoned Dónal was on the beer.

"You were looking for me Ned?" Dónal said inrerrupting Fallon's attack.

"I was. Where the fuck have you been? Have you your phone turned off or what? No one has seen sign or sound of you for ten days or more. What's happening out there?"

"My phone fell in the water out in Mussafah. I got a new one but there was something wrong with the connection. I sent you an e-message nearly every day. Did you not open up your mailbox?" Dónal asked, knowing Fallon had never gotten to grips with the medium.

"Don't talk to me about e-mails. Tell me about the Dredging Company. Some fellow called Prince or Fritz has been on to us here. He wants us to price up a huge project out there. He was talking to Gordon. He says he will only deal with you. Is he for real? Who is he?

"That would be my old friend, Faisal. He is head man now for NMDC. I met him recently and he cleared our rig through the port chop chop! We go back a way. He even invited me to his house. Well, when I say house I mean palace. He is related to Sheikh Hamdan. A nephew. He knows how I work. We get on well."

"This is a big project. We've not seen the details yet but it's bigger than anything we've ever had before. Much bigger. You would have to head it up. ADNOC will finance the project but we, you, that is will manage it. Our men, our method" Fallon said.

"You mean "my men, my method" I think", Dónal replied, putting Fallon on the back foot. "If I'm to do this I'll do it my way, without any interference from you."

"You'll have to set up another company out here with me as MD and joint owner" Dónal continued, applying the pressure, "you wouldn't have a smell at a job like this without me and you know it. I reckon I could pick up the phone to Faisal and have him offer the work to myself if I wanted to."

"I said before that I trained you too well Dónal but you're asking too much. You're being too fucking cheeky now. Too greedy."

"Too right Ned" Gordon chirruped in the background.

"Shut that idiot up and get rid of him. The game is changing Ned. I could blow you right out of it right now. All it would take is a phone call. So 50:50 or I go it alone. And don't attempt to make a move on my visa. Faisal will rearrange one in minutes. 50:50 and we walk away afterwards, quids in!"

"All right, all right. It's a deal. Subject to our being awarded the works. I'll draw up an agreement and send it to Ali. Mr Shawkie will have to be involved."

"No. Keep Ali & Sons out of this. Everything will be done through NMDC. End of."

"We'll have to talk this through. I'll over there in three or four weeks and we'll sort it out than. We'll sign the contracts then."

"By "we" you mean "you and me" I take it and not you and Gordon.

"Yes, it'll be just us two. But you better not fuck it up. There's a lot at stake here.""

"Smart move, Ned! I think maybe it was me who trained you too well!"

Chapter Nineteen

COCHIN

Their time in the resort passed quickly and without incident. Keralese houseboats, similar to the local working boats but refurbished for the tourist market, came and went, mooring at the hotel jetty. The resort was on an island, joined to the mainland by a narrow causeway and on the second day Ravi brought Dónal for a tour on the minivan, as much to check its roadworthiness as for any other reason.

The long road from the island to Cochin ran parallel to the river, separated from it by miles of wharves and dockside warehouses. The road was busy, mainly trafficked by large forty foot trailers with the TATA logo on the front of the tractor unit. Their minivan was also made by TATA, as were the taxis and most of the cars they passed. Most, if not all, of the warehouses, also bore the TATA Legend.

"We're in the real India now boys. No doubt about it. Did you ever see so many people? All hustling and bustling. And the dust. It's everywhere. How do they stick it?" Phil asked.

At every pause or stop the minivan was approached and surrounded by begging children, tapping on the windows and pointing to their mouths to signal their hunger. Some of the children were crippled and skipped towards them on crutches, others were disfigured and some had the shortened hands of thalidomide poisoning.

"Do not on any account whatsoever open the window or hand those beggars any money or we will be completely and utterly drowned under them. They are professional beggar types and anything you give them will end up in the lining of the pockets of their owners."

"Their owners?" Phil said, "You mean their families, like the gypsies and tinkers we have back at home."

"No, no Mr Phil. Most definitely not. Not their families. Their owners. Their families will have sold them as these children will not ever be married and if no marriage then no dowry for a male and another adult to feed if a daughter cannot be married off. A good beggar will always earn money for his owner. No doubts about it. The owner will look after the beggar because the beggar makes money for the owner."

"But why don't the families look after them?"

"They are ashamed Mr Phil, ashamed. Many years ago a family would have thrown the afflicted child into the river so as to hide their shame but the government stopped this practice so now there are many peoples with polio and impetigo and all sorts of diseases. The families sell these children and the beggar gangs move them around to good begging spots all over India. Sometimes they are making the affliction worse as the beggar will earn more if his body is all twisted up. It is terrible but in India it always been this way."

"I don't believe that. Sure no parents would sell their afflicted child into slavery like that."

"Unfortunately it is so Mr Phil. Many people in India are very poor and living in small villages where the people are very ignorant. Other people in the village would make life hard for the family. They would most certainly be evicted. People would not want an unlucky family living amongst them."

"What about their religion? Does that not forbid such practices?"

"For a Hindu or a Jain Buddhist then it is a matter of fate and so it is not their responsibility. For a Christian, selling the child is not allowed so the child would perhaps be placed in an orphanage or a hospital and forgotten about. The beggar gangs might bribe the manager of the orphanage people to release the child or arrange an escape. But that is not the fault of the parents. The same is true for good Muslims but bad Muslims, who knows?"

"Here in Cochin and in the South it is not a big problem really. The beggars in the street vill not be starving but in Delhi and in Mumbai and in Calcutta the problem is very much greater. But even there nowadays no one is starving. People are very poor but they get by whether by begging or collecting plastic bottles or other rubbish no one else is vanting and selling it. Indians are very enterprising people. It is the way of things here."

"For example in Mumbai, like I told you the children dig the mud from the drains to get the tiny particles of gold. Also in Mumbai the children work near the municipal slaughterhouses where the animals are butchered. No one is wanting the guts of the animals so the muslim children collect them and clean them out by boiling. Along the riverside then they hang them out to dry first blowing them up like long balloons. They sell them to a local company for export to Europe where they are used for foodstuff packaging to make the German sausages."

"Many people in India have little education and are very ignorant. But the slum dwellers manage to survive. Chai wallahs and rickshaw wallahs bring tea and transport people in the hope that one day someone will be bringing tea to them or they will be the passengers and not the pedaller. That is how it vorks here. Everyone dreams of becoming rich."

"I'll never eat another sausage or piece of black pudding as long as I live" Phil said "this place is the pits. How can people live in this filth?"

"It's beyond me but they do" Tony agreed "but do you notice something? I spotted it before and I see it here as well. People are in some way or other happier here, more content with their lot if you know what I mean than us. The have-nots don't seem to resent the haves – they just want to get on themselves."

"I don't know about that" Dónal said. "There must be some level of discontent here. Didn't you notice there are police on nearly every corner?

"Aye" said Phil "and the slogans stencilled on the walls alongside the communist signs. It would remind you of Derry or Belfast."

"The communists are very strong in Kerala" Ravi added. "Many cities have communists in the councils and there are many Communist Party of India Members of Parliament but at the end of the day all Indians are Indians first and will put their religions in front of politics. A Hindu Communist should have the same ideals as a Jain or Buddhist or Christian Communist but of course that is not the case at all. No sir By Jove. Not in India. That is not happening."

Dónal raised an eyebrow at this mini outburst. He had often reckoned Ravi had an agenda of some sort. He had figured Ravi had maybe some personal ambition to better himself by whatever means but he had not expected this departure. Ravi was the model of the self –effacing Indian servant, ever polite and deferring to his master. But he had just revealed something of himself. Perhaps he had misread Ravi. Was he a political animal after all?

"If the communists had full control" Dónal said, baiting Ravi "then all they would do is take the wealth from the rich and divide it up until everyone was poor. They would keep all the top jobs for themselves and their cronies and the country would be impoverished like happened in Russia and Eastern Europe. I remember the Berlin Wall coming down and I worked in Poland when it was an EU Accession state. The people there had nothing under the communists, nothing only hardship."

"That was only because those countries never recovered from the sacrifices of the war and were held back by the western powers. One million Indians fought in that war and what did they get? An India partitioned and governed by the Brahmin Hindu. That's what we got. Muslims forced to Pakistan and Hindi forced south. Each side attacking the other and burning one another out in a power struggle between Jinnah and Gandhi. And when it was all over, Sayeed still had to pull a rickshaw and Kapil still had to wash the entrails out. Both slaving all day to feed their families. They were no better off than off under The Raj." Ravi countered.

"So you would support the Communists then Ravi? A man after my own heart! "Revolution now and down with the running dogs of the imperialists" that's what I say. You agree?"

"Please Mr. Dónal. Forgive me. I spoke too freely. I am not political. Politics doesn't put food on the table for anyone but the politicians. But I must admit my blood is boiling over when I sometimes think of how poor some people are while others are so wealthy. I am a Christian. A Hindu or a Muslim or a Buddhist would perhaps not be as concerned. But I think change is necessary most definitely and I think the communists might make that change."

"You might be right Ravi, you might be right. But for now we need to eat and buy some clean clothes. Cheap stuff will do the job. Bring us to a market and we'll see what we see."

"You will better off eating in your hotel or in some other fine establishment" Ravi said "as the food preparation will not be hygienic outside of such. The street food and cheap cafés are not suitable for you. You will all have Delhi Belly. The water here on the streets will not be clean. It will be very dirty. Great works are being proposed to bring clean water and sewers to our cities but unfortunately there is a long way to go before it will be acceptable. I am used to it but if I am in Abu Dhabi for a time where the water is clean I am getting sick when I return to India.

You must only drink bottled water and always check the seal is intact before drinking as some fellow will be putting bad water in used bottle. Even if the seal is good there is no guarantee the bottle is not a forgery as unscrupulous people are putting dirty waters in false bottles. It is the way of things in India. It will never change."

"So we can't drink the water, we can't eat the food. Can we have a beer? What are the bars like?"

"The bars for you are in the hotels and restaurants. Indians buy the alcohol in toddy shops where homemade illicit spirits are sold. Toddy is wine from palm juice and alcohol. It is like strong beer. Also there are the official government licensed shops but often the whisky is not real Johnny Walker but is a fabrication. Same for gin. Only Indian beer here will be all right maybe sometimes. Believe me Mr. Dónal, you should confine yourself to the hotels for the eating and drinking. And do not on any account consort with any of the women there as they will be prostitutes and full of disease."

"We're getting an education today no doubt about it boys" Dónal said "and this is the rich part of India. Bring us to that department store and we'll stock up on gear for the coming week."

Ravi did just that and in a huge crowded seven floored shop they stocked up with armfuls of fake designer clothes – shirts, socks, shorts, underwear, jeans, hats and caps. The whole lot cost a pittance and Dónal pointed out to the lads all the accessories and trinkets on sale – the same stuff as was on the street stalls at home at one hundred times the price.

"Now you know how they can do it at home boys" Dónal said "and these people make a profit! How much do the poor misfortunate creatures who have to sew these clothes up make?! I read one time how women were blind from trying to do the needlework all day long from dawn till dusk just sewing sequins on shirts. It's crazy, shameful!"

"That is true, all that is true" said Ravi "but if people didn't buy the products then there would be no vork for them. The solution is to pay them a fair wage and allow them work in good conditions but the factory owners are wanting always to maximise their profits and that is the very root of the problem. Yes, the absolute root and cause of it."

"Most people in India are very ignorant Mr Dónal. Binda and Moussa and the other workers we have in Abu Dhabi are very ignorant men. The same is true of most of the Pakistani workers there. That is why educated Indians and Asians who can read and write are occupying all the office jobs and those ignorant fellows are working on the construction sites as labourers and drivers and other menial positions."

"So what is the solution Ravi do you think?"

"Well I believe in the very first instance we must get rid of the corruption in all the governments of India. That will mean demolishing the Civil Service which has in effect been in charge of the country since before the British came and has been in charge since they left. They take bribes and live in comfortable houses near the railways and work in the office for only a few hours every day. The politicians and the civil servants work hand in glove with each other to uphold the system along with the police and the army. They all live in comfortable bungalows in special areas in every city set aside for government and municipality and armed forces people. They have houseboys and servants and drivers like the sahibs and meme-sahibs of old. New Delhi was built for them exclusively so they would be able to live apart from the real people in the city. It makes me mad to think about it!"

"Fuck me Ravi" Dónal said "I've never heard you talk like this. What's gotten hold of you?"

"Normally in Abu Dhabi I am not saying boo to a goose but conditions in India make me always angry. I am angry and I am ashamed. I am ashamed that my people would prefer to continue to live as slaves instead of overturning the bosses. Everybody in India has the right to vote but the people sell that right every time to the candidate who gives them cheap whisky and a party at festival time. My blood is boiling because of this and a thousand other injustices."

"It is the same all over the world Ravi. Life everywhere is a struggle."

"People do not lie down in the street to die or be eaten alive by rats in London. They do not have to work for fourteen hours cleaning the sewers to earn enough for a bowl of cheap rice. They do not have to fear their daughters will have to sell themselves for a few rupees every night to a disgusting old man or a filthy dirty kitchen porter. There is a difference between struggle and slavery. In India if you are born poor you are born a slave."

"Hmm. I see where you are coming from Ravi. Perhaps once we finish our work here you will have enough to maybe improve the situation a little."

"A little? Yes, perhaps but a little will not be enough. I assure you even a lot will not be enough to reduce the scale of the problem. It is just so very big. So very big. Only by a total revolution will the problem be solved. That is what is needed By Jove Yes. No doubts."

They returned to the hotel where they had some food and relaxed for the rest of the day. Dónal called Angie and spent ages on the phone to her. It was good to hear her voice. She offered to fly out but Dónal told her to stay put. He told her about all he had seen and of his misgivings where Ravi was concerned. She asked him about Mr. Saki.

"Mr. Saki will help Dónal. I think he can be trusted. There is something honest about him."

"You might be right. If he is anything like Gian then he can at least be trusted. But he will need to be paid for his trouble. Still Saki could be our insurance in all of this. I'll think some more about it. Tomorrow we go inland and uphill to Munnar. If Ravi is as good as his word we will sell our bars of chocolate there, turn around and come straight back to Cochin."

"Be careful Dónal. Please be careful. Money isn't everything. I love you and I don't care that much for all this luxury. I've had my hair done, my nails done, my body buffed and am all worn out from all this sunshine. A wet afternoon in a pub in Sauciehall Street with you by my side seems very attractive just now. Very attractive."

"You're dead right there pet, dead right. I don't know why I took this on. Greed. That's all it is. I can tell the lads are fed up with it as well. The last two weeks on that boat put things into perspective for all of us."

She was right of course but they had come this far and there was no going back now.

Chapter Twenty

MUNNAR

The country immediately outside Cochin was a revelation. Ravi had often spoken of how green a land Kerala was but nothing had prepared the lads for the lush, cultivated, farms and plantations they passed through. They drove by flooded fields and paddies and saw workers transplanting the green shoots of the growing rice and other cereals.

Further along, above the flood plain, the terrain was greener, populated by row upon row of cultivated palm. "Rubber trees" Ravi said and sure enough when they looked more closely they could see the incisions in the tree bark and the resin collection cups affixed.

"This is one of the finest rubber plantations in the whole world" said Ravi in his tour guide voice, "this plantation is operated by Mr. Tatta and the rubber is produced here and sent to Tatta Tyres for use on Tata Motorcars. The workers here own the plantations in many different cooperatives. They are always looking at the rubber price on the stock market and Mr. Tata pays them in accordance with the price. It is a very good system here. In other Indian States there is different system in play but that will change also with time."

"And what caste are the plantation owners Ravi? Dalit?"

"This is difficult to explain, Mr Dónal. Caste is a Hindu thing. It is not about money. You see there are poor Brahmin and rich Dalit! Within each caste there are classes depending on wealth . An upper class Dalit will be wealthy but will still be a Dalit."

"And what about the Christians? Your people?"

"With Christians it is the same except that there is no Caste being allowed or recognised but there is a class difference no doubt about it. You will see this if you stop at any of the Christian churches on a Sunday. Everyone is wearing their Sunday best and the people who dress up the best and sit at the front will be the biggest contributors while the poorer people will be in saris and sitting at the back. But all are welcome and a good priest will not recognize any difference."

"Same as at home" Phil said "no difference whatsoever."

"What amazes me is the number of churches. Since leaving Cochin there has been a church of some denomination or other at every crossroad. Roman Catholic, Greek Orthodox, Syrian Orthodox, Anglican, Coptic, Methodist. Then the temples, Jain and Buddhist, Hindu and Muslim. The place is worse than Ireland. Worse even than Northern Ireland!"

"India is a very spiritual place Mr. Dónal, everyone here has a faith of some sort or another. Here, even atheism is considered to be a statement of faith. Along with the more established denominations there are many Amahs and Gurus who are carrying on religions of their own with many followers here and all over the world on the internet."

"Someone somewhere is making money off the backs of all these believers" Dónal said. Organised religion is indeed the opium of the masses, eh Ravi?

"Most certainly that is true Mr Dónal. You are familiar with the words of Marx. But a true radical must allow for individual faith and make that faith serve the revolution. Too often revolutions serve the faith and that is where any why revolts have failed."

"This is getting too deep for me Ravi! How long to Munnar?"

"Maybe only two hours now. I will have you converted and indoctrinated by then" Ravi said, laughing loudly and enjoying his victory in the debate.

After an hour or so of driving through crowded towns and villages in the low hinterland of Cochin the road began to climb upwards into the foothills of the Western Ghats and with the climb the terrain, the vegetation and the climate changed.

The dry dusty heat of the city was left behind and the lowland plantations came to an end as the road wound ever upwards along the contoured land following the natural clefts and ridges of the hills. The air became damp and heavy, as though about to rain.

They passed through dense hardwood forests and logging camps where huge sections of the woods had been stripped bare and were now in the process of being replanted. Efforts were clearly being made to renew the woodlands but hardwood trees such as mahogany and teak took a long time to grow and when the forests were first exploited little thought was given to their renewal but the government had set aside vast areas of the remaining forests, designating them as National Parks where no logging other than controlled culling was permitted.

There were many lay-bys on the road which doubled as public viewing areas where travellers cold park and take in the vista. A number of Hydroelectric schemes had been undertaken and the dams and reservoirs so created were advertised and proclaimed on huge signs complete with arrows pointed to the various features in ken.

Roadside toddy houses were at every bend and clearing where local men could be seen alongside the entrances drinking and talking or playing what looked like dominos. Again, Dónal was stuck by the numbers of people, even here in the middle of nowhere.

"Where do all these people come from?" Dónal asked Ravi.

"Oh these people live in the villages in the forest everywhere. Some are working in the forest. They are taking fruits and nuts and all sorts of herbs and spices and selling them or mixing them into potions and medicines for the alternative medicines and Ayuverdic therapy for massaging and all sorts of cures for all sorts of ailments."

"Do they work?"

"Oh yes Mr Dónal. Many of our medicines are sold all over the world in both conventional and alternative medicines. The drug companies pay for many forest products and sponsor research projects. Cures for everything are being discovered here all of the time."

"Also of course many of the people work in the tea plantations and tea blending factories which you will see momentarily as we approach Munnar. The local women mostly pick the tea and the men work also in the collection and processing. See, look now."

And with that, as if to order, they rounded a bend in the road and saw valleys covered with a carpet of green bushes, neatly laid out in blocks, within which a small army of sari-clad women carrying huge sacks on their shoulders were to be seen gleaning the top leaves from the bushes.

"It's like the PG Tips ad!" Phil said.

"So this is where all the tay we drink comes from. Why do we say "all the tea in China" then if it comes from India?" asked The Badger.

"Now there hangs a tale" Dónal said. "It goes back to the Opium trade. The Emperor in China had banned opium but the Brits reintroduced it to pay for tea which was only available in China and Japan. Then they stole some shoots and transplanted them to India. I'm sure it's more complicated than that but that's the gist of it."

"It was an Irishman who identified this part of India as being suitable for tea, believe it or not! Lafcadio Hearn was his name. Bit of a chancer but he travelled all over the East. Ended up in Japan. I read about him yonks ago but had forgotten all about him until now."

"That is not all Mr. Dónal. Oh no! Much of the machinery for use in the tea blending factories was in fact manufactured in Ireland in the very same place and by the very same company as built The Titanic. I have seen it myself oh yes indeed. I have seen it myself!"

They passed by a sign for a hill station where accommodation was offered.

"Many people come here and spend some holidays here staying in the old plantation houses. Since Mr. Tata has now taken over nearly all of the plantations and the blending factories the old hill stations where the tea farmer lived have no purpose any more so the owners have made them into small hotels. But it rains a lot up here. Very dangerous then. The mud is being washed onto the roads and cars crash all the time."

They stopped at a lay-by to stretch their legs and take some photographs. Dónal kept an eye on the traffic following and took note of a Toyota Landcruiser that pulled in up ahead of them. No one got out but Dónal counted four turbanned passengers.

"Sikhs! Mr Singh's men!" Dónal said to himself, "hopefully, we won't need them but it's good to know they're there if ever we do."

He watched Ravi to see if he had clocked the minders but he gave no sign of it if he did. Ravi looked a bit jumpy however, constantly taking his glasses off and polishing them. But that was nothing new in itself. He was always fidgeting, always scratching some part or other of his anatomy. Always tugging at his trousers or adjusting his balls.

"Soon now we vill be in Munnar Mr Dónal. The trader is just across the bridge in the town. The town itself is full of hucksters and holy men. Saddhu. Be sure and give them a small token or they will be making a fuss and cover you with blue dye. Some will be dressed like monkeys as this is the festival of the Monkey God. It is a nuisance but this is India by Jove."

"Will your man have the money Ravi? It is a very large sum we are after."

"Oh yes. I have made enquiries already. The cash will be ready for us. Then I suggest we hightail it back to Cochin as fast as the breeze will go. No staying overnight up here. Once we have the money we should go."

Munnar was smaller than Dónal had expected. The town was split by the river and the streets were full of the usual bazaars. They were hungry so Dónal stopped while Ravi went into a store for some Mars Bars to keep them going. Dónal turned to the others while Ravi was out of the jeep.

"There are two roads out of this place to Cochin. I checked the maps earlier. Ravi brought us along the better road. I reckon he'll make his move on the way back. Tourists and heavy traffic take the circular route and return on the other road. That's why we met no busses and little traffic coming against us on the way here. Ravi will want to return to Cochin that way but at the last minute I'm going to turn about and head back the way we came. I might be wrong about him but we're going back on the opposite road to the one he chooses."

"I can't figure him our either" Phil said. "All that talk about revolution! I figure he's in league with some bunch of radicals or other. Give him some money towards his cause by all means but not a full share."

"Here, he's back! Watch him but if he says take the low road, we'll take the high one!

On setting off again, Dónal asked Ravi whether they had to go back on the same road as they had come.

"Most definitely we should go back the same way Mr Dónal. The other road is longer and goes first to Aleppy before turning to Cochin along by the backwaters. It is at least two hours more for driving along a busy road full of lorries and busses and all sorts."

"Fair enough. Take us to the money man so!"

Another half hour of driving and Ravi asked Dónal to pull in at a roadside filling station. There was a small covered area there where men, truckers from their appearance, occupied plastic chairs and drank tea from glasses while arguing amongst themselves.

To the rear was a parking area and Ravi motioned Dónal forward towards and around the trucks standing there. Behind the trucks, hidden from the view from the road and the café was a Toyota HiLux.

Dónal stopped the jeep. Ravi got out and walked over to the Toyota. Its windows were blacked out so Dónal couldn't tell how many were within but he guessed four.

The driver's door opened and a huge, huge as in fat, Indian alighted from driver's seat of the truck. "How in the fuck does he fit behind the steering wheel?" Dónal said "He must weigh the bones of thirty stone. He'd be the father of an almighty shit."

The others sniggered at that, releasing the tension.

"He wouldn't be must use in a tunnel, right enough" said Phil, "unless you wanted to keep him at the bottom of the pit to prevent flooding. He could be wedged into a four foot pipe and not a drop of water would escape."

"Shut up the fuck" said Dónal "if that fat bastard thinks we're laughing at him there's no knowing what will happen."

"What's he going to do?" said The Badger, "fall on us and squash us to death? Look, they're coming over. Little and large!"

The larger man walked to their jeep as Dónal got out. The others remained seated.

"This is Mr. Gupta Dónal. Mr. Gupta this is Mr. Dónal."

"Allow me to begin Mr Dónal. I have long experience in the matter of concern and I am more familiar with the procedures which are very simple and straightforward. Please call me Gupta" the Indian man said, in perfectly accented English.

"No peasant here!" Dónal thought as he replied that he was happy to do as directed.

"First I will examine the merchandise and verify the quantity and quality. This will take no time. My family has been buying and selling gold for many generations and I will know immediately if the goods are, as you say, the business."

"For your nine bars", he continued, "I am prepared to offer you a fair price. Not the market price as it is simply so high no one can touch it at present. But a fair price, non negotiable.

Today, a fair price for one hundred and twelve and one half kilograms of gold of uncertain provenance, whether hallmarked or not, is, in cash, two million United States Dollars. Take it, or leave it. I suggest you take it. You will not get any other offer in this locality."

"Gold is at a very high rate just now. You will double your money overnight." Dónal replied.

"I expect to. I fully expect to. But how I do that is my business and of no concern of yours. I am taking your risk, your burden from you once I take the gold. You should consider that. Anyway, do we have a deal or do we go our separate ways?"

"I will put your proposal to my partners Gupta", Dónal said and with that he went back to the jeep for a conflab with the others.

"This guy is going to hand over two million US for our stuff. It's not what it's worth but it's a fair shake. Will we take it?"

Both men nodded their agreement. "Just get rid of the stuff Dónal. I want to sleep comfortably in my bed again." The Badger said. A sentiment the other two easily identified with. "Take what you can get and we'll get the fuck home."

With that Dónal returned to Gupta's motor and reached out to shake his hand.

"You have a deal Gupta. You have a deal."

"You have made a good choice Mr. Dónal. You will be able to walk away from this problem now while I will have to deal with it from here on. I wish you luck. Now drive your jeep closer and we will make the exchange."

It was a simple as that. Gupta's men took the gold while Dónal took two carrier bags full of dollar bills of various denominations. Dónal had no way of counting all the money there and then. Nor could he tell if it was good money or bad. He picked up some bundles of $100 bills and flicked through them but it could have been monopoly money for all he knew.

"It is all there Mr Dónal and it is all good" Gupta said. "Business is business. I would have to kill you, a European, if I was to cheat you and that would mean investigation of my affairs on too many fronts. Your man Ravi knows this."

They shook hands at that and went their separate ways, neither pausing to look back.

"Now Ravi" Dónal said, "point me in the direction to Cochin "we're home and dry."

"We'll be home and dry when we're back in Abu Dhabi" said Phil, I'll not be counting any chickens until then. And neither should youse."

Chapter Twenty One

AN UNEXPECTED STOP

Dónal watched Gupta and his crew departing before setting out for Munnar and Cochin.

"I'm thinking we might return on the other road lads. It might take an hour or so longer but we'll have a change of scenery until Aleppo."

"That road is not so good as the road we came here by" Ravi said "there are very few places designated as passing places and there will be foul ups and all sorts and we will be going against the main flow most of the time. The other road is better in my opinion. Also it is much shorter."

"Still, we'll never again be here so we might as well see some more of the countryside."

With that he took the left fork on the road at Adimali for Thekaddy. Glancing in the rear view mirror he could see the jeep he had clocked earlier shadowing their progress.

"Our minders" he said to himself "probably no need for them now that we've taken the other road against Ravi's wishes but better safe than sorry! Still at 25% it's soft money!"

Progress was slow. The road was narrow in places and wound its way down from the uplands through verdant countryside. Traffic was light. Most of it was headed in the opposite direction to them and they went from one game of chicken to another as truck driver after truck driver refused to give way until the last possible moment, many of them grinning fiendishly at them as they passed, almost shoving the jeep off the road. Most of the truck drivers seemed to use the white line, where one existed, to centre their vehicle instead of keeping to one side of it!

"This is very dangerous road Mr Dónal like I was telling you. Often the truck drivers will be falling asleep or will have been in a toddy house. The trucks go over the cliff and people are being killed all of the year."

Sure enough, as they rounded one of the many interminable bends a small truck was skewed across the road, blocking it. It looked as though it had skidded into the crash barrier.

"That's all we need" Dónal said as he slowed the jeep, stopping some twenty metres back from the stalled vehicle.

He checked the rear view mirror before reversing further away from the truck but the following Land cruiser had closed in right behind him and was parked across the road, blocking him in.

"You must give me the keys now Mr Dónal, the game is up" Ravi said "I am sorry to inform you the Kerala Liberation Army has greater need for the bags of the money than you do."

A number of men, armed with pangas and machetes rushed out from behind the truck. They were joined by the occupants of the Land cruiser who were similarly armed.

"Not Sikhs!" Dónal thought, his hopes dashed as he realized these guys weren't his minders. "I should have known. These fuckers are too small!"

"Please all of you. Get out of the jeep now. "This instant" Ravi ordered "if you do as I say you vill not be harmed but do not try anything silly as these fellows will slit your throats without even batting their eyelids a single time."

"I knew all along you were up to something. I never trusted you" Dónal said as he struck out at Ravi, hitting him in the face with first his right then his left then his right again before he was set upon and restrained by Ravi's men.

It took three of them to pull Dónal to the ground, pummelling him as he fell and kicking him as he hit the beaten clay.

Phil and The Badger made to weigh in on his side but the now alert gang held them back, waving the machetes inches from their faces and landing a blow to Phil's shoulder, slicing into the flesh causing him to yell out.

"Leave it out lads" Dónal said from the ground "It's over. Let them have the money. It's not worth dying for. Leave off and we'll get the fuck out of here alive."

Ravi's nose was pumping blood and he was trying to stem the flow with the filthy snotty handkerchief he was forever wiping his brow with.

"Now the shoe is on the other foot Mr. Dónal. But you are right. These men would most happily finish you all off. No one even knows you are in India. Killing you all would not present any difficulty whatsoever as you are not officially here and if you are not officially in India then you cannot be officially missing. You will officially be missing in Abu Dhabi of course but that is of no matter. No matter entirely. We could kill you this very instant and leave your bodies in the forest and that would be the end of the matter. And the end of you also." Ravi laughed.

Dónal was seriously questioning Ravi's sanity in his own mind when procedures were interrupted by the arrival of a brace of Mercedes. The cars were driven right up to the Land cruiser and four tall, fully bearded, turbannned, Sikhs leapt out of each car. The eight men approached. Each carried a gun, either a handgun or a shotgun.

The leading Sikh aimed his pistol at the Land cruiser and fired twice, blowing the front tyres out. Another aimed and fired over the heads of Ravi's crew. Some words, Hindi, most likely were shouted by the leading Sikh and Ravi's men as one dropped their swords.

The Sikhs moved quickly, rounding up Ravi and his gang, herding them off the road and into the forest while helping them along the way with vicious kicks and punches. They searched them and relieved them of any cash. They took their mobile phones and their shoes and left them barefoot in the pine needled forest carpet.

"What the fuck's going on now?" Phil said "are we being robbed a second time?"

"No. No, thank fuck!" Dónal said. "Not being robbed. Rescued, boys, rescued. These men are on our side. They are Mr. Saki's men. I took out some insurance in Abu Dhabi. I've saved your bacon yet again!"

One of the men, the leader, ambled over to Dónal, placing his panga into a scabbard to signal friendship.

Dónal held out his hand and the Sikh took it and shook it vigorously,

"Mr. Saki sends his good wishes. My name is Kris Singh Kumar. We have been keeping our eyes on you since you left Cochi. We will accompany you now to Kottayam where a plane will collect you. Mr Saki fears your Ravi will watch the seaports so he has arranged a plane for you. Please take this telephone and he will tell you this himself."

Dónal took the phone "Mr. Saki" he said "is that you?"

"No Mr Dónal. Sorry to disappoint you. It's only me. Your Glasgie Gal."

"Hey Ang! Wow? How are you? I've missed you, We've had some time here. Some adventure! But we're heading out soon. Mr.Saki came through. I thought we had lost the lot but his guys came and bailed us out."

"I know, I know. He tracked you all the way. You owe him big time. Not least because he looked after me while you were away. And you owe his brother in Southampton."

"And you" he said "I owe you. I owe you big time. The thought of you kept me going through all of this. We have lots to sort out once I get back. I love you babe, I can't wait to see you. I can't wait to hold you."

"I will look forward to that Mr Dónal" said Saki, laughing. She must have handed him the phone. "But first you must get back here safely. We have angered some very dangerous people. Kris is my nephew and is to be trusted, I wanted to tell you this myself to reassure you of his credentials. Do not delay in Kerala, keep moving. People will search for you when that Ravi does not report in to his superiors. You will be all right I am certain but do not delay. As soon as that creature gets to a telephone they will try to seek you out. They will suspect that the broker Gupta has had a part in this so they will certainly visit him first. This will buy you time but not much. Gupta is one of their own. He is too fat to endure pain."

"That's reassuring. Nice of you to see the funny side!"

"If there is no laughter then there is no life Dónal but you already know that I think. And without life there can be no love, so, in a roundabout way, laughter is what makes the vorld go around, not love."

"Too deep for me Saki. That's way beyond me. Put the boss on again."

"I'll see you soon Ang. We'll be out of here in a matter of hours" he said as Angie picked up the phone "then we can go forward. We have so much to talk about. So much to plan. So much to do. And we'll follow Saki's deep thinking and have at least one laugh every day".

"We'll need more than a laugh a day, if you get my drift."

"And a smile then. I promise to put a smile on your face each and every day for the rest of your life. In sunshine or in shadow, wet or dry, hot or cold, I will make sure and certain that you have a laugh and something to smile about every day for the rest of our lives if you will have me, that is."

"Sounds like a proposition that. Well, if it is, then the answer is "yes". Yes, I will marry you. Just get back here now. Chop chop!"

"Orders already? We're not hitched yet you know."

"Maybe we won't be if you don't haul ass" she laughed.

"Sounds like a "Jeldi Jeldi"order to me Dónal" Saki cut in, "you had indeed better haul ass!"

Dónal said goodbye at that and handed the phone to Kris, thanking him and his crew for the part they had played in the drama.

It took them less than two hours to get to Kottayam where the small jet chartered by Saki stood on the apron, awaiting their arrival. Kris handed Dónal the bags and before boarding the plane Dónal took ten bundles of $10,000 and handed them to Kris.

"Please share this among your crew as you see fit Kris. We are all in your debt. This money will I'm sure come in useful for you and you families."

Kris looked at Dónal for a moment, measuring him and for that one moment Dónal was afraid Kris might take offence at the offer. Was it not enough? Too much? Inappropriate?

"Your offer I accept as one friend to another. I will always be your friend Mr Dónal. I sense goodness and honesty in you and in your companions. If you ever chance to return to India and if you ever happen to visit The Punjab I am to found at this restaurant owned by my brother in Amritsar" Kris said, handing Dónal a card.

"I might just take you up on that Kris" Dónal said, "and sooner than you might think."

With that they all shook hands in turn, the rescued acknowledging their rescuers. Even though it was Saki who had organized things it was Kris and his men who had provided cover on the ground. They had earned their cut.

The lads boarded the plane, taking the two bags into the cabin. As soon as they were settled in the plane taxied out to the runway and took off without delay. On reaching cruising altitude the plane levelled off and a liveried steward came through from the cockpit, opened a bottle of champagne and served them with each a glass with the compliments of Mr. Saki.

"We made it boys", Dónal said, raising his glass "we made it!"

"We're not landed in Abu Dhabi yet" Phil said "but it's near enough, near enough I'll grant you. Aye, near enough to be good enough" and with that he too raised his glass and drank from it, his face grimacing as he tasted the fine wine "but a pint of stout would go down far better than this piss. Or a drop of rum. That's your man, a nice drop of Captain Morgan by the fire on a cold wet night with the rain and the sleet beating against the windows of the pub and the lights flickering in the squalls. I never thought I'd say it but there's a lot to said a bit of wet weather. Sláinte boys!"

"Slán" Tony and Dónal responded, downing their drinks and recharging their glasses, smiling at one another and relaxing for maybe the first time since that night in The Angel, a lifetime away, it seemed now.

"It's been some journey no doubt lads, some journey. Four short months ago I was farting about making money for Kingdom Tunnelling and going out every night getting shitfaced.

Spending every penny on booze and chasing women. Nothing achieved and no ambition to achieve anything other than to get laid or maybe own a decent car some day."

"Then we find the gold, the bars of chocolate and everything is changed. We've not used the money yet but already my life has been changed by it. I'm not bothered that much about booze anymore and I think there has to be more to life than the life I had. Do you know what I mean?"

"Maybe you're growing up Dónal" Phil said. Tony will tell you we were stone mad until our late twenties and we only got sense when we got wed and had the bairns. You're not the first man to puke up last night's beer down a tunnel and you won't be the last. Isn't that right Tony?"

"He's right Dónal. You're being too hard on yourself. You just needed to grow up a bit and I think you've done a fair bit of it of late. And it's not all down to the gold. That wee lass Angie has had a big influence on you lad. She is the reason you've changed. She's the real gold in your life. Whatever you do, don't lose that particular treasure. You'll regret it if you do."

Chapter Twenty Two

PARADISE FOUND

Six months later found Dónal and Angie in Abu Dhabi celebrating New Year in the villa they had moved into following their marriage on Dónal's return from his Indian adventure.

Angela was expecting their first child and Dónal was more excited about it than she.

The work in Mussafah was at an end and Phil, The Badger and Jimmy were in Ireland, The Badger on the farm he had bought and Phil in Burtonport in the house he had built overlooking the harbour where his trawler lay moored at the quayside.

Dónal had expected he would settle for a life of indolence but he found it very hard to adjust to idleness when, true to his word, Faisal contacted him.

Faisal had fixed things for Dónal, appointing him lead Contracts Manager on all major port developments to be undertaken by NMDC both in The Middle East and further afield. Dónal set up a company, "Gold Standard Construction", which was recognized throughout Dubai and Abu Dhabi as the only firm which treated its Asian workforce with dignity and respect and was held to be a model employer in this regard.

Jimmy had remained on with him as a sort of general factotum and man in charge of chatting up nurses. He preyed on the newer arrivals and looked to be willing to go the distance. The others had set him up with "enough to be going on with" as Phil had put it "but not enough to kill him".

Angie devoted her time to setting up a charitable organization devoted to the education and betterment of the Dalit orphans and street dwellers of Cochin. The organization was entirely funded from the sale of the bullion and was called "Golden Opportunities". She loved the commitment and she loved the very worthwhile and fulfilling work involved.

On Christmas Eve Dónal and Angie were sitting on the beach in Abu Dhabi.

"This is the first time in I don't know how long that I've not been shitfaced by this time on a Christmas Eve" Dónal said as he sipped some tea. He reached over and kissed Angie. "And I have you to thank for it. For all of it. I do love you Ang. So much you can't know".

"Och I do know you idiot I've always known. I knew it afore you knew it yourself. Now why don't you ring the lads. You know you want to. They'll be waiting for your call. Go on, make the call."

With that he called The Badger at home.

"Well skin" he said "is it easy now?"